I0691200

A CANDLE, A KISS, A CHRISTMAS GIFT

A Long Way Home Novel

RAYMOND S FLEX

THE BUS-STATION WAITING ROOM

J*ason Jeavons* didn't much feel like going home for Christmas. Funny that it only really hit him—like *really* hit him—when he heard the gut-wrenching *shriek* of the automatic doors to the bus-station waiting room closing behind him.

But he was here now.

He *was* going home.

No two ways about it.

The warmth of the bus-station waiting room was somewhat overwhelming. It was that greasy, pulsating heat—the kind of heat that brings the pores out in a lather. The stuff which, if you were really that way inclined, you could use to baste turkeys.

Jason could still taste the remnants of the onion-and-lentil soup he had ingested seconds before hurtling out of the door. He could still smell the acute scent of the onions. He imagined himself almost like in a cartoon, the smells coming off him in scribbled, inky-black waves.

1

Jason tugged the hood of his sweatshirt up over his head, and he peered out at the state-of-play in the bus-station waiting room tonight.

Collection of weirdos.

But what had he expected? This was Christmas Eve, after all.

Who in their right mind travelled on Christmas Eve?

Yes, Christmas Eve; that semi-sacred period which meant compulsory Family Time, and overindulgence in *everything*. By all rights, Jason should've been back home, with his family, slouched up in the battered armchair in the corner of the sitting room, doing his best to stay out of the passive-aggressive squabbles of his parents.

It would be the same as last year.

It would be the same as *every* year.

His mother would want to flip the TV to some 'romantic'— and usually black-and-white film—while his father would be determined to watch one of those abhorrent Yuletide editions of some panel show: the ones with the borderline, supposedly ironic—*and-yet-still-quite-racist*—jokes; and with the big-titted cleavage of whichever particular 'model' they'd chosen to be that year's host.

It had almost become something of a self-harming ritual.

Jason would lie back, in said armchair, and he would time how long he could stand it before he felt like his head was going to explode. He didn't fire up any sort of stopwatch app on his smartphone—*nah*, he wasn't that committed to the thing—but he would simply keep an eye out for the wrongly set LCD clock on the DVD player. The clock was so far out of whack, and had been that way for so long, that Jason now subconsciously knew

2

that 7.13 a.m. really meant 4.01 p.m., and that 11.47 a.m. really meant 8.35 p.m.

Eight hours and forty-eight minutes between the false time and the correct time, and yet Jason could perform the calculation almost instantaneously.

He wondered, in more masochistic moods, whether this time change had happened due to a power cut or because of one parent or the other's passive-aggressive attack.

Jason wouldn't rule out either.

Both were just as likely.

Yep, Christmas was a really special kind of misery.

And Christmas Eve was just the beginning.

Jason took in the waiting room, all spread out before his eyes, and he was almost blinded by the too-bright, fluorescent, strip lighting for his trouble.

A *really* weird group tonight, though. Looking about their faces—*dear Lord*, their *clothing!*—was a real eye-opener.

Take the guy sitting closest to the door, for example, how he seemed to be wearing something which Jason would've termed lederhosen, but he was just as confident that he was wrong. No, at university, he had elected computer science, not history, for a reason.

Computer science was dependable.

Sturdy.

A clear-cut career path.

No surprises.

No *illogical* surprises, in any case.

Jason moved his glance along the lacquered wooden benches to the next person waiting.

A woman . . . no, that probably wasn't the right word for her .

. . and there was the reason why he hadn't gone for English either. Simply put, words made Jason's head ache.

And that was without going into detail about what they did to his stomach.

No, this was—*most certainly*—a 'lady'.

The *lady* wore a feather boa and what Jason thought to be a white, mink coat. The sort of outfit that somebody might wear for a night out at the theatre, but certainly not to sit about in a bus-station waiting room.

Not even on Christmas Eve.

When Jason had allowed his gaze to linger for too long, the lady glared at him with a real fury. Though Jason's social graces really weren't up to much, he could certainly tell just what it meant when somebody shot him one of *those* glances.

Jason looked away.

This time, he found himself looking over a young man—about his own age.

What marked the young man as odd was how he was wearing a chicken costume. The chicken costume itself was a collection of dusty—was that dust?—scraps of material which served as the 'feathers'. The chicken head took its cues, apparently, from a balaclava, and had been sort of dyed a shade of corn yellow—not *ripe* corn-yellow, no, more of a where-did-the-locusts-get-to? corn yellow.

The young man, to Jason, looked just a little green about the gills, not that Jason was much of a good judge: he was a teetotaller.

Something else was off about the young man in the chicken suit, though Jason struggled to put his finger on it. Something about the boy—about his costume and his complexion—seemed somewhat golden . . . golden, was that really right? . . . at least that seemed the only way of explaining it.

Finally, Jason took in the elderly woman who sat crouched in the corner of the waiting room.

She wore a thick, navy-blue duffel coat—all the toggles done up—with a thick, rainbow-coloured scarf about her throat. She was hugging herself tightly and if she wasn't *actually* asleep then she was certainly doing a very good job of imitating the action.

Jason never would've allowed himself to doze off in a bus-station waiting room.

Not even on Christmas Eve.

There wasn't anybody else in the bus-station waiting room. It seemed that it would just be Jason and these nutters.

Jason glanced up at the flat-screen monitor—encased in a chicken-wire mesh—and saw that his bus; headed to Staplesham —was delayed indefinitely.

This just got better and better, didn't it?

About half an hour ago, on a whim, Jason had come to a sudden halt with his current pet project: a program which measured the amount of time—and words—somebody spent on their email during the course of the day. Oh, sure, he had no passion at all connected to the project, but he saw people buying up all this boring-as-hell software crap constantly.

So there had to be a market for something so mundane.

And, anyway, once he got through with his computer-science degree he would need to get used to a whole shit-ton of boring projects.

There was nothing much fun about where Jason was going.

About where he would end up.

Anyway, Jason had been rattling along on 'PROJECT 164'—

he hadn't even bothered to give it a name it was *that* dull—when he'd had this extremely odd tingling sensation, right down at the base of his gut. At first Jason had thought it was appendicitis— he *always* thought it was appendicitis—but then he had snapped back to his senses, told himself that, most likely, he was just hungry.

Hunger . . . hunger? . . . nope, that wasn't it either, he had chomped his way through a veggie burger only an hour before the feeling had arrived. Just to make sure it wasn't hunger, he had prepared himself the onion-and-lentil soup.

Now he found himself thinking through what the veggie burger might've contained:

Beans.

Soya.

Tofu.

Something like that.

Sometimes—being a veggie—Jason did wonder if he should maybe pay a little more attention to just what was in his food. He was fairly certain the veggie burger hadn't contained meat . . . not as a principle ingredient at least . . .

Once Jason had vanquished the hunger theory, he'd shifted through to other needs and wants.

And he'd come up short.

When he'd flitted right through everything he might've possibly eaten that day, which might've caused this particular sensation, he decided to head on with the abstracts. Which was to say, as far as Jason was concerned, those desires which fell outside the spectrum of his physical body.

And he knew it.

He *just* knew it.

Knew what it was that was bugging him.

Jason cast his mind back to that defining moment. He had just dealt with what had been working itself into being a very nasty—and poorly placed—infinite loop. For the briefest of seconds, call it a sort of celebration for this sad, little triumph, he had allowed himself a short glimpse at *Newsbytes*: his favourite news-slash-computers-slash-comedy news source.

And there it had been.

The Advent Calendar.

That corny, ironically rendered thingy with so many moving parts it made his eyes hurt simply to imagine it inside of his own mind.

And the calendar had been opened to Christmas Eve, which, in retrospect, seemed like a fairly reasonable place for it to be.

But that was what had touched Jason.

What had gripped him by the gut and turned him inside out . . . not to put too fine a point on it.

Jason cast his mind back to the Advent Calendar. To the moving-gif-image thing which'd stared back at him.

It'd been obscene.

Of course it'd been obscene.

That was the whole point of the Advent Calendar—the whole thing had been a *kitsch-fest*.

The image which'd appeared that day on the kitsch Advent Calendar had been of a boy—a *man* really—about Jason's age. Within the gif image, the *man* had been lugging a rucksack all the way up the driveway of a snow-plastered home. He was all rosy-cheeked and there was a broad smile smeared across his lips, which was where Jason was glad to lose the resemblance for good.

As the gif went on, the man continued on his way up the snow-covered path to the home.

There was something of the Creeping Death about it, really. Now that Jason thought about it.

That completely *inevitable* feeling that the boy-slash-man *would* end up on the doorstep, and then, of necessity, go through that front door.

And so why hadn't Jason seen it coming?

It had surely been obvious enough.

And—yet—it had affected him.

Affected him down low.

In the pit of the gut.

Because, as that front door opened wide, and as the beaming family looked out on their returned offspring, Jason had been close to crying . . . or as close as he was *ever* going to get.

The gif had faded toward the end, and the large splash of violet and yellow showing the message: 'MIDDLE CLASS TURDS' hadn't so much as raised a smile in him.

And then Jason had set about checking on bus departures.

That was how this whole mess had got started.

Fucking nostalgia.

Jason huddled himself up in the corner of the waiting room opposite the old lady in the duffel coat.

He grabbed his rucksack to his chest tightly and continued to feel that steady quiver of anticipation through his guts.

His rucksack was the same battered old one he'd had all through school; the one with the half dozen zip-up compartments of which now only one of them still possessed the capacity to be zipped. Thankfully, it was the main compartment. The other compartments just all sort of flubbed open in pure, unattractive, charity-shop chic.

Jason could feel the reassuring shape of his travelling computer within the rucksack. It was much older than the system he used for his studies. About five years older. The reason that he hadn't carted his whole setup along for his impromptu trip back home for Christmas was really threefold:

One: This had been a whim.

Two: His main system was *enormous*.

Three: He was unnaturally paranoid of getting mugged . . . and while Jason would've liked to say it was because all his university work was on his main system, the closer truth was that he couldn't *bear* to lose the system itself.

All right, if it came right down to the quick of the matter then he would admit it happily.

He was in love.

It was Computer Love.

He was in love with a machine.

Even inside of Jason's own mind it sounded wildly irrational. But he didn't care.

And it wasn't like there was some woman in his life—or *man* as some of his 'mates' occasionally enjoyed intimating . . . no, there was nobody to compete with his Computer Love.

Perfectly healthy, then.

The warmth in the waiting room was overbearing—or had Jason really taken his relationship with his computer to another level?

Was he *fantasising* about it?

About being *among* those sizzling-hot chips . . .

He ended his thinking right there.

Jason had opted for a clunky pair of nearly unworn hiking boots he had bought for an ill-fated camping trip in Wales.

It had become ill-fated because the trip had never come about.

One of those plans which would always get talked about without ever coming close to being implemented.

But despite the trip being nothing more than an ethereal mist, the boots very much had their uses . . . at least, Jason had felt extremely sure-footed on his way to the bus station.

He had got here in one piece, hadn't he?

Hadn't he?

. . . Well, he was alive.

As Jason glanced about the waiting room, and then back to the caged TV screen, he caught onto an odd feeling. He analysed it a moment. Tried to work out what his subconscious was getting at.

There was no alteration to his bus's arrival status—but that was to be expected.

Good things *never* happened to Jason.

Buses never simply *showed up* on time.

And certainly not earlier than scheduled . . .

Jason's attention was drawn from the stasis of the waiting room.

The automatic doors were drawing back.

Somebody was coming in.

Another passenger.

Well, a new *prospective* passenger.

For a couple of seconds, Jason's breath just stuck in his throat. He felt himself tremble.

All over.

Jason took her—because there was no doubt that she *was* a 'her'—in.

He couldn't say that he had ever noticed women all that much, but he certainly noticed this one.

She wore a pair of light-blue jeans, a thick bomber jacket on top, and a pair of *really* busted-up old trainers. The tail of her beige-cream shirt stuck out at the hem of her jacket.

She carried a large rucksack over her shoulder—at least twice the size of Jason's rucksack—and she glanced about the waiting room, briefly crossing eyes with Jason. She seemed to be looking for someone—someone who she had arranged to meet.

As she sat down on one of the wooden benches, she immediately dug about in her rucksack and produced a pair of wrap-around headphones which she promptly snapped into place over her ears . . . it was as if she wanted to *ensure* that nobody in this waiting room would so much as *attempt* a conversation with her.

To be honest, Jason couldn't blame her.

Jason had to look at least *half* as weird as the rest here.

He *had*—if only in his mind—been reflecting on his potential Computer Love.

And here he was now.

Leering.

But Jason didn't care.

He couldn't take his eyes off of her.

He examined the way her fine, golden hair hung down the side of her face, leaving only the very tip of her ears to poke out.

She had her hair up in a ponytail—drawing her hair back from her pearl-pink skin.

Jason had to admit that he was enamoured . . . if the English language would allow him that particular observation.

Was he going to do anything about it?

Probably not, going on *definitely* not.

But it was the thought that counted.

The fact he was no longer thinking about the relative sexual attractiveness of his computer surely had to count for something.

Jason broke off his—slightly obsessive—gaze at the girl.

He glanced back to the screen showing the bus departures.

Still no sign of the bus going to Staplesham.

When Jason brought his gaze back to the spot in mid-air before his nose—and got to wondering whether he might be able to sneak a peek at the girl again—he found himself locking eyes with the elderly woman who wore the duffle coat.

She was awake after all.

He tried to look away.

But she had him now.

The way that a wizened old woman can so easily crush an unsuspecting young man with only a single look. And she pinned him with it now.

Jason couldn't have looked away if he'd wanted to . . . and, come to think of it, he actually *did* quite want to.

The woman held his look, and then said, quite cleanly and unambiguously, "Stop time!"

"Huh?" Jason reasonably responded.

The woman continued to glower at him.

Her light-green eyes seemed to seethe right through him,

burning him just as thoroughly as any nuclear isotope worth its salt.

Then, all of a sudden, her eyelids clamped shut once more. And Jason no longer had to deal with that glare of hers.

Somewhat relieved, Jason looked away from the woman. He turned back to the bus-station waiting room. To his fellow 'waitees'.

They were all as before.

Waiting patiently.

The man in the lederhosen.

The woman with the feather boa.

The young man in the manky, old chicken suit.

And, of course, the princess, the diviner of dreams, Jason's own personal goddess:

The girl with the golden hair.

Jason looked between them all.

And every one of them—without exception—succeeded in avoiding his gaze.

Jason supposed that if he'd encountered himself in a similar situation he, most likely, would've done the same thing.

However, as Jason swept his gaze back around the waiting room, his eyes somehow crossed those of the man in the lederhosen. He now saw that he wore a Bavarian hat, too . . . or what Jason would've *termed* a Bavarian hat.

Nothing could be done.

The man gave Jason a firm nod of the head. Then he rose from his spot on the wooden bench. Made for the automatic sliding doors of the waiting room.

For some reason, Jason found himself wanting to follow the man in the lederhosen. It was as if something within was speaking clear and loud. So that he couldn't ignore. Or maybe he just wanted to get some air. It *was* stifling inside the waiting room and the others would most likely relish his disappearance if only for the moments in which he was gone.

So, watching the automatic door to the bus-station waiting room slide open, Jason got up from his seat on the wooden bench and headed after the man dressed in the lederhosen.

Although Jason was by—many measures—a social retard, he wasn't naïve enough to leave the rucksack containing his computer behind in the waiting room.

That particular *travelling* computer might not really have anything except sentimental value, but it would be deeply annoying if one of the nutters scarpered off with it just because they could.

Beside anything else, it would knock something of Jason's macho pride.

And there was *precious little* of that to start with.

The air seemed to have grown chillier when Jason stepped out through the sliding doors, his backpack slung over his shoulder. He immediately brought his hands up to cover his cheeks against the cold. He basked in his own warmth for some moments and then he shifted his focus to the man in the lederhosen.

Jason could make him out—standing ahead on the road. He was smoking something—a cigarette?

Jason caught that shifting, restless sensation down in his gut once more and he realised that he was surely doing something which was socially unacceptable.

He stopped staring.

He turned his back on the man in lederhosen.

On the night air, Jason smelled the tobacco smoke drifting over to him. Jason had always secretly quite liked the smell of smoking—and what was cooler than some hero, or villain for that matter, lighting up a cigar or cigarette, or *pipe*, in a film?

"I thought you would never arrive," the man in the lederhosen called out, in a distinctly Germanic accent.

Jason was stumped for several moments, and although this tended to happen to him all the time—in pretty much every 'social situation', or 'conversation' as the rest of the world appeared to refer to them—on this occasion the stumping was especially present because of all the *baggage* which had come before.

There had been all that weighty, unsaid shit back in the waiting room.

Jason had—apparently—put his foot in it with this—probably quite nice—German gentleman. And he was—seemingly; in a second-language sort of way—referring sarcastically to Jason's stalking of him.

Was Jason stalking the man?

He couldn't rightly respond yes or no.

The German man in lederhosen continued to eye Jason closely. He held a cigarette—one of those ones with a holder—which continued to smoulder away between his fingers. "Well," the German man said. "You have nothing to tell me?"

This time—*somehow*—Jason managed to find his voice. He went with a definite, if slightly uncertainly phrased, "Yes?"

The German man frowned. He paused for a moment, parted his lips, and Jason—realising the confusion—caught up with himself.

"Ah," Jason said, "actually, I meant, 'No, I don't have anything to tell you—it was a double negative, or I didn't want to make it a double negative"—again, imaginings of English teacher reprimands loomed over Jason and he realised that he was better off cutting his losses—"but all that aside, I just wanted to apologise for having followed you out of the waiting room—really it was a misunderstanding. Only I felt cooped up in there, almost unable to breathe, you know . . ."

There was a pause while the German man in lederhosen appeared to absorb what Jason had just said.

Jason decided to save him the trouble. "Forget all that," Jason said, turning away. "Just please find it in your heart to forgive me —that's all I ask."

Jason had managed to get a grand total of two steps away before the German man called him back . . . and that led Jason down yet *another* uncomfortable stream of imaginings.

Had the German man in lederhosen somehow interpreted Jason following him as a 'come on'?

Because it felt like Jason had already dealt with a whole host of crap on Christmas Eve. To have to deal with a declaration of love—let alone running nose-first into a long-dangling question mark over his own sexuality—might somehow tip him over the edge.

He set a determined stride for the, now-closed, doors of the bus-station waiting room.

Jason stood before the doors. He waited for the motion-sensitive sensors to kick in.

But they didn't.

As Jason peered in through the scratched-up, cloudy glass, he could make out the others within. Jason considered banging his fists against the glass. But before Jason could put any such plan into action, he smelled the thick tobacco smoke on the air, and he turned to see the German man in lederhosen bearing down upon him.

With a slight amount of surprise—and perhaps a touch of fatalistic despair—Jason saw that the German man in lederhosen was smirking at him.

"You cannot return inside," he said.

Jason felt his heart clench as tight as a fist.

"You must take me home, first," he added, as if this made everything make sense.

As if it made everything okay.

It didn't.

In fact, it only seemed to push Jason—*finally*—into taking any sort of significant action on his situation.

Jason bashed his fists against the glass of the automated sliding doors.

Nobody stirred within.

He tried again—this time louder.

Nothing.

Not so much as an arched eyebrow; the flicker of a disapproving glare.

No reaction from the 'lady' with the feather boa.

Nothing from the man in the chicken costume.

No change to the sleeping old woman's expression . . . the one who had enigmatically cried, "Stop time!"

Now she slept on.

Perhaps the non-reaction which hurt Jason the most was the girl with the golden hair. She simply bobbed her head slightly as she listened to her headphones. Off in her own world.

Was Jason still in his own world?

It would be nice to think he still was, but the quickly accumulating evidence appeared to point in another direction.

Jason eyed the German man, that smile still very much a part of his lips. "You do not understand anything, no?" the German man said.

"No," Jason agreed.

The German man gave a slight nod—nothing more than the gentlest of inclinations of the head—and he said, "*She* did not think to explain a few of the details?"

"No," Jason replied, finally feeling as if he was getting somewhere . . . or perhaps he was just raising his hopes for nothing.

He had been mistaken before.

Often in fact.

"She did not think to explain *who* you are?"

"No," Jason answered, glumly this time, and then, not wanting to seem like the total dunce this German fellow had no doubt pinned him as, he added, "My name's Jason Jeavons. I study computer science."

But this vague attempt to save face backfired in the form of another smirk from the German man.

Jason didn't quite understand how he had succeeded in keeping his mouth shut for such a long time only to make such a spectacular fool of himself when he did eventually—*inevitably*— have to open it.

Still, at least the German man, if he did find this situation amusing, didn't see fit to continue the joke.

"You are very special, Jason Jeavons."

"Am I?" Jason replied.

"Yes, you are what one might say to be *one in a million*."

" 'One in a million', " Jason replied, thinking to himself that he had never—*ever*—thought that he was anything other than *bang* average.

"One in a million," the German man repeated back, as if this was an important point to grasp. Then he continued, "Unlike the majority of humankind, you have a very *strange*—very *unique*—power, Jason."

Jason kept his lips sealed this time, although he did have the urge to fire back a "Do I?"

"You have the ability to communicate with the Unquiet."

"The Un-what?"

"The Unquiet, Jason."

Jason supposed that his latch-jawed expression was enough to tell the German man that he was thoroughly befuddled.

The German man smiled—didn't *smirk*, thankfully. His tone was a touch disbelieving the next time he spoke. "You really have never heard any of this before, have you?"

Jason shook his head.

"You have never noticed the dead—never have you seen the ghosts which inhabit your own world?"

Again, Jason shook his head.

Thinking that he should say something—*anything*—he blurted out, "I spend a lot of time with computers."

Jason *did* wonder to himself how he had managed to get through life without noticing the ghosts and, even after some long —*searching*—thought, could not come up with so much as a single satisfactory reason.

Then again, what he had said about spending a *lot* of time

with computers was certainly true . . . and he wasn't so blind not to realise that it *did* block out some parts of the world.

The *human* parts mostly . . .

Still—*shit*—twenty-one and just having found out that he could see ghosts. It was a pretty heavy state-of-affairs to deal with.

If it was even true at all.

Who was to say that *any* of it was really true?

Perhaps this German man was some nut, just a crazy person wandering about.

A threat to himself as much as to society.

Should Jason make a call to the appropriate emergency service . . . what even *was* the appropriate emergency service?

. . . What if the German man wasn't even real?

What if Jason was simply conjuring him up from within his own mind?

This all really was food for thought.

And yet, the German man—in all his leder-hosened glory—did stand before him here and now . . . if only inside of Jason's mind. Perhaps Jason should just do whatever the German man said. It wasn't like anything bad ever happened to people who listened to the voices in their head—not in *real life*, surely . . .

Jason glanced back in through the closed automatic doors to the waiting room.

The cigarette smoke was so thick in Jason's nostrils now that he might've closed his eyes and imagined he was standing beside a bonfire.

Beyond the glass, Jason could make out the others—the waiting passengers; the people who he'd all *thought* to be passengers. "Are they all dead?" Jason asked the German man.

When the German man spoke this time, his voice was firm, and Jason could tell without so much as glancing back at him that he wasn't smiling or smirking now.

"Yes," the German man said. "Tonight—Christmas Eve—it is a special night in many cultures. A night of giving; and receiving."

Jason turned away from the waiting room, but not before he'd had a good eyeful of the golden-haired girl within.

The German man continued, "As a Channeller—"

"A *what?*" Jason said, already instinctively concerned whenever he was called anything he didn't understand.

"A Channeller," the German man went on, "is a Mortal soul who has the ability to communicate with the Unquiet—with those who have unfinished business; those who never completed their life's path as intended. Those who—left to their own devices—over the course of many centuries; perhaps thousands of years; might well become corrupted by the despair of what they have perceived themselves to have lost and turn what remains of their life force to wicked means."

The way the German man said 'wicked' set a chill tingling down Jason's spine. "You mean . . ." Jason trailed off, hoping this might prompt a fleshing out of the explanation, without confirming himself as a *complete* moron.

He was in luck.

"Yes," the German man continued. "Poltergeists, goblins, little devils in the dark; they have many names among Mortals and they all amount to more or less the same thing. Those which —to the common man—appear unexplained. Bitter, twisted interactions between this world and the next." The German man stuck his finger up in the air as if he might be making some point or other at a political debate. "But Channellers possess the ability to calm these spirits—to allow them to pass on. Into the next world. Their work done."

"So, that piece about Christmas Eve being a time for giving and receiving; *I'm* the one doing the giving?"

The German man *did* smile this time and he gave a slight shrug. "Well, they do say that giving is a form of receiving."

"Yeah," Jason said, looking about to see if there was anybody nearby potentially observing him conversing with what might appear to be thin air.

As luck would have it, there was nobody about.

A JOURNEY TO ANOTHER TIME ... IN LEDERHOSEN

J*ason allowed* the German man to lead the way.

It seemed the only sensible course of action since Jason had next to no idea what was going on, and, for a spook, the German man seemed pretty clued-in to just how things worked.

Soon enough, though, as the German man explored his past history—went into detail about how exactly he had come to snuff it—Jason realised that the German man had had *more* than enough time to work out the ways of the world.

Not to mention the afterlife.

An odd thing happened as Jason lagged back from the German man.

At first, it happened out of the corner of his eye, and then, before he knew it, the sight was unavoidable.

Dawn was coming.

Creeping its way up from the horizon.

Bathing the buildings in its glow.

It was times like these when Jason wished he had a wrist-watch . . . or that his smartphone wasn't stashed away in his rucksack, slung over his shoulder.

Still, he was fairly certain that it was eight o'clock in the evening; for whatever good perception did him. He was certain that dawn wasn't *scheduled* to arrive for another twelve or thirteen hours at the very least.

And yet, here it was . . .

Jason was quite aware, as they trod along the pavement, that the cement had quickly shifted away from its familiar ditch-grime grey. Now it was a sandier shade, and—somehow—less substantial than it had been before.

The German man had offered Jason a mint as they'd been striding along, and Jason had accepted.

As he sucked on it now, he found his thoughts switching in and out with the rise and fall of the minty waves moving through his cheeks and tongue.

Ghosts—*Unquiet* . . . he supposed that he had always hoped he might be exceptional in some way. And yet, he had always quietly nurtured the idea of 'exceptional' as meaning one of those autistic mathematicians.

Jason's deepest, darkest dream had been to be a rogue—no-rules-for-me-thanks—universe-bending mathematician.

But things hadn't panned out that way.

He had ended up going into code-monkeying when he'd got back the latest results for one of his maths modules.

Reality was a bitter pill to swallow.

When—acting on an adrenalin high having just got back his results—Jason had decided to confide his wildest of dreams in the 'Career's Guidance Officer' at his school, the Career's Guidance Officer had deigned to give a slight, wry smile and suggest he try 'something else'.

That something else had ended up being computer science; seeing as Jason had done remarkably well on those particular tests.

Jason snapped back into his surroundings.

He couldn't help but notice that the buildings which'd previously surrounded him—the late sixties 'monstrosities', as his more architecturally aware father might've pointed out—had transformed into far more elegant, curving forms.

With far more wooden beams and thatched roofs than Jason ever might've bargained for.

And another thing was the density of said buildings.

Whereas before buildings had littered the foreground and then kept on going all the way back as far as the eye could see; now they pretty much only occupied the sides of the main road which ran through town.

When Jason glanced up, he could catch sight of the hills which grew up on both sides of the town. Lush green hills, with the odd sheep or cow, here and there.

For a solid set of moments, Jason paused on the heels of the German man so as to get a proper look at his surroundings . . . they were, well . . . there was no other way to describe them . . . *wonderful*.

This was so far away from being a 'concrete jungle', as one critic of this London satellite town had described it, as could be imagined.

The whole town . . . or should Jason have better termed it a village? . . . was actually rather *quaint*.

Jason could only make out the cottages at the sides of the road, flowers blooming up over stone walls and through trellises. It was actually something of a *glorious* morning.

And none of the wintery chill remained.

Almost like it was . . .

"Middle of summer," the German man said, his words drifting back over his shoulder. "That was when I died."

Because Jason felt like he should say *something*, he said, "Was it?"

The German man just plodded onward.

Jason observed the German man as he slipped through a break in one of the stone walls. The pavement, or whatever had been underfoot, gave way to the muddy path of a field.

Immediately Jason felt the wet earth suck at his walking boots and he was extremely glad that he'd gone for the footwear he had.

Sometimes trusting his instinct was the very best thing he could do.

Sometimes.

The German man continued along the muddy footpath of the field until, after clambering up a slightly slanting piece of terrain—Jason was hesitant to call it a 'hill'—he found himself standing at the top of a downward-leading track.

The track led on down to a flattened section of field in the middle of which was pitched a circus tent. The tent itself was a whole cacophony of colours: reds, blues, greens, yellows . . . mauves, teals, tangerines . . . who *really* cared about colours, anyway?

Jason followed on the heels of the German man still some-what confused about just how day had dawned so quickly; and *asymptomatically* . . . at least Jason hadn't *noticed* the German man slipping a chloroform-soaked rag over his airways . . . but, then again, Jason might not be either seeing or hearing—not to mention *feeling*—anything particularly well this morning-slash-evening.

Jason *supposed* this would all be some sort of a hallucination. But, if it was, then just what was Jason supposed to do about it?

Pinch himself?

Slap his own cheeks?

No, if Jason truly *was* a Channeller—and he hadn't quite convinced himself that he was—then he was determined not to be a foolish one . . . or to at least stave off giving the impression that he might be a foolish one to the population of the 'Unquiet' until the last possible opportunity.

They plunged on down into the field and Jason did his best to keep up.

He could feel sweat trickling down the collar of his shirt and could smell the salty, sticky odour coming back to him. He wondered if he maybe should have taken a shower back before he'd left his halls of residence . . . too late to turn around now.

The German man refused to break pace for even a moment at the entrance to the circus-style tent—or was it a marquee?—and he headed right on into the shady interior.

Jason went after him.

The air inside the tent smelled stale and, strangely, of potatoes.

Almost as if the German man had read Jason's mind, he turned back and muttered, "The circus people sell potatoes on Sunday mornings—it is a good secondary source of income."

"Hmm," Jason said, looking around. "I can imagine."

The inside of the tent was incredible.

There were empty spectator seats surrounding the arena on all sides—nothing grander than wooden benches. The centre of the tent, where Jason was standing right now, had been covered in several layers of sawdust.

Potatoes wasn't the only smell in the air.

There was *manure* too.

The source of which became evident when, hearing a percussive set of footsteps, Jason turned to examine the entrance at the other end of the circus marquee.

An elephant.

Of that, Jason was certain.

All things considered, there was really nothing at all *subtle* about an elephant.

The elephant was led on the end of a frayed rope by a diminutive, Indian-looking boy.

At least Jason *took* him for an Indian.

The boy wore a white linen shirt which dangled all the way down to his knees, and he had a bleached-white turban wrapped about his head.

"Andercheth," the German man said, apparently referring to the Indian boy for Jason's benefit.

The Indian boy continued to lead the elephant around on the end of its rope.

The elephant inspected everything gathered about the periphery of the arena with its trunk.

Something about the elephant wasn't quite right. Even Jason, not having the first *clue* about elephant behavioural patterns noticed that.

Maybe it was the way the elephant would come to a sudden, definite halt every dozen or so steps.

Stir its forefeet in the sand.

Shake its head.

Its tusks.

The only way the elephant could be calmed was for the Indian boy to slip quietly up beside it and whisper gentle words in its—*fairly substantial*—ear while he massaged its trunk.

Jason watched on as the Indian boy led the elephant back out of the arena; and he noted how it commenced its nervous stirrings once again.

The German man turned into Jason, and said, in a dispassionate voice, "That, my friend, is my destiny; my fate." He then paused for the longest time and when Jason caught the German man's face in profile, he realised that he had a tear in his eye.

"My *death*," he pronounced with stone-faced finality.

BEFUDDLEMENT

The *German man* shifted on out of the tent soon afterward. Jason, assuming he needed to follow the man in order to get back to his own life—*his own time* . . . his own world?—trailed him.

The two of them walked for a long while between the smaller tents and the odd horse-drawn carriage. Neither of them spoke.

Finally—and it really *had* been a long while by this point—the German man turned to Jason, no trace of the tears now, and said, "I never told you my name, did I?"

"Nope," Jason replied.

The German man stuck out his hand. "I am Dougleglass Schmidt."

Jason gave the German man . . . *Dougleglass Schmidt's* . . . hand a good shaking.

Realising that he'd missed the social cue—*as always*—Jason reciprocated. "Jason Jeavons," he said, and then feeling something of a wry twist entering his mind, he added, "At your service."

Dougleglass smirked in that vaguely friendly way of his.

Once they'd walked on some more, Dougleglass came to a sudden halt outside one of the tents.

Dougleglass reached out and took hold of the canvas between his fingers, fondling it for several moments in the same way a child finds comfort in their favourite stuffed animal.

He glanced back at Jason and said, "I need to fetch something from inside here."

With that—somewhat brief—explanation, Dougleglass vanished into the tent.

Jason stood about outside, not really knowing what to do with himself while he waited.

Across the field, emerging between tents, he spied a pair of young women—about his age; or perhaps that was just wishful thinking. The two of them wore skimpy leotards. These, Jason assumed, were the tightrope walkers, or the gymnasts, whoever it was who would be strutting about on that balance beam back inside the main marquee.

As they brushed past Jason, the two of them fluttered their eyelashes.

They both had ebony hair and lips painted a raw red.

When they'd taken several steps beyond Jason, and ended up back inside the marquee, Jason found himself breathing in pungent lavender perfume.

Turning around, Jason was a touch shocked to find Dougleglass suddenly at his elbow; a sly grin lining his lips. Jason saw that he was clutching something.

"I should not get involved if I were you," Dougleglass said.

"And why's that?" Jason replied, surprised at the sharp tone he struck; as if he had *had* any plans at all to 'get involved'.

"One of them might be your grandmother."

"What do you mean?"

Dougleglass threw up his hands to indicate their surroundings, or it might've been out of simple exasperation. "The past!" Dougleglass said. "I am from *many years* in the past."

Jason felt an unpleasant stirring in the pit of his stomach. He thought back to the pair of sable-haired girls. He hadn't *recognised* either of them as possibly being his grandmother . . . and it was fair to say that she wasn't *reported* to have been a tightrope-slash-balance beam walker.

Then again, Jason supposed every family had its secrets.

If he was honest, if Jason had been able to look beyond his grandmother's mounted-up wrinkles, managed to get past the stench of elderflower which continuously clung to her; would he ever have *accurately* have been able to imagine how she might've looked at his own age?

Probably for the best to take Dougleglass's advice, though.

Better to be safe than sorry.

Dougleglass was smiling all over again. He tapped his temple with a pair of his fingers. "That got you thinking, did it not?"

"Is this *really* the past?" Jason asked.

Dougleglass gave a slight wince, as if he was in physical pain, or perhaps his mind was doing battle with space and/or time. "Yes, and *no*," Dougleglass finally replied.

"Explain," Jason replied.

Dougleglass jabbed his tongue hard into the side of his cheek in a way which—Jason was certain—could only communicate Very Deep Thought.

Jason prepared himself for a truly earth-shattering, foundation-shaking, world-eating revelation.

"It is sort of like the past—but a *spiritual* representation of the past."

Jason blinked.

Twice.

Then once more for luck.

"That . . . that's it?" Jason said. "The *Spiritual Past?*"

Dougleglass nodded dolefully; his exasperation apparently beyond description. "That might be one way of putting it, yes."

Jason looked at Dougleglass evenly, and then shifted the weight of his rucksack over to his other shoulder. "I think I can just about get my head around that."

THE SPIRITUAL PAST

Dougleglass *went on* to explain to Jason that anything he did here—in the Spiritual Past; a sort of past for the ghost world —would have no effect at all in Jason's own time . . . that when the old woman in the duffel coat had barked out, "Stop time!" at him, with little or no explanation, she had meant it really quite literally.

Dougleglass also said that, once he got through with helping him, Jason would return to the waiting room.

Jason had to admit now that—whatever reservations had gripped him before—he was actually quite looking forward to getting home for Christmas.

As Dougleglass spoke with him, Jason couldn't help but keep looking at the photograph which Dougleglass gripped in his fist. The one which he had dug out of the tent. A couple of times, Jason managed to actually get a glimpse of it, but it was one of those old-style, sepia-stained photographs that really required—

all things being equal—a magnifying glass in order to be able to examine it thoroughly.

Dougleglass turned into Jason and said, "Are you ready to help me—to show me the way back?"

Jason creased his forehead into wrinkles. "The way back *where?*" he asked.

Dougleglass held the photograph up. He showed it to Jason. "The way back to *her.*"

Jason examined the photograph.

It was pretty much as he had thought of it previously, which was to say that it was somewhat tricky to make out any of the features. The sepia tones made the task near impossible.

But Jason did his best.

From the photograph, Jason could tell that Dougleglass's girl-friend—because that was surely who she was—had fair skin, rosy cheeks, and blond hair. She wore a sort of half smile, as all the people from around this period seemed to . . . at least in all the history books which Jason had been forced to leaf through back in his schooling days.

Jason supposed—right here and right now; in this particular moment in the Spiritual Past—it was somewhat costly to have a photograph taken. That, to some extent, accounted for the well-thought out composition, and the otherworldly gaze of the girl looking off into some unseen—*and unseeable*—spot in the distance.

The thousand-yard stare.

When Jason glanced back up from the photo, Dougleglass looked to him with a vague grin and said, "Let me tell you about my death."

Really, it seemed that Jason had very little choice in the matter.

Dougleglass took them back through the rows of tents, and through the sticky, black, sodden mud.

Jason could smell human waste on the air—piss and shit—and he supposed that waste management wasn't quite what it was in his own time.

Especially a travelling *circus.*

Thinking about it, that elephant alone must've accounted for a good proportion of the strain put onto local waste management systems. Not that Jason really cared, of course. All that kind of stuff was a little too Real World for his tastes.

Jason dealt in bits and bytes, and he was infinitely glad to do so.

Just the prospect of having to wade through Real World shit got his brain meshing and whining.

Dougleglass said nothing more till he brought Jason to a larger tent; not half as large as the main arena, but bigger than most.

When Dougleglass peeled back the tent flap, Jason immediately felt a waft of warm air hit him.

And then there were the smells.

Rich, sizzling onions.

A thick scent of salt.

And the rich odour of meat stew.

Jason could just about feel his stomach quivering with anticipation. He felt a cool wave pass through his chest—and through his blood.

Jason was pretty heavily accustomed to his university diet which consisted of any combination of noodles, pasta or carrots . . . he really couldn't be much bothered with anything else; he knew where he was with those foods. And yet, even though Jason had been a vegetarian for the entirety of his conscious life, he couldn't help but feel just a few hunger pangs at the prospect of the meat stew he could see bubbling away over in the corner.

But then he snapped out it.

He thought back to those images of the beef slaughterhouse which he had seen in that video documentary *way* back . . . back when he'd been a kid.

That was the thing about the internet, and especially for a child, there were so many things out there which—simply put— once seen could never be *unseen*.

The inside of the tent was lit by a series of flickering candles and although it wasn't an especially cold day outside, the warmth from the fire blazing away in the kitchen was welcome.

In the end, with Dougleglass guiding him along, Jason decided against pushing his luck with the meat stew. His body couldn't handle any sort of meat at all after all these years—he had found out as much when, in a fit of hunger and culinary experimentation, he had snatched up one of the spring rolls which had come with one of his friend's Chinese takeaways, and had administered an unrepentant bite.

Jason had discovered, after several minutes of vomiting, that there hadn't been all that much vegetarian about said spring roll.

The whole experience had actually served to put him off experimental alimentation—not to mention *meat*—indefinitely.

And now, after all that had gone on, and with a—no doubt —*delicate* stomach, this wasn't the time to think again.

So, instead, Jason settled on an innocuous-looking bread roll along with some rich and well-churned butter.

Together, Dougleglass and Jason sat down on one of the rustic wooden benches.

Jason quickly finished his bread roll and settled in to observe Dougleglass making inroads into his portion of meat stew.

As Dougleglass consumed his stew, he spoke to Jason.

"In this place I was a juggler—that was my role." He glanced up briefly from his soup. "This place is called the Jensen Brothers' Circus—*Swedes*," he added with a touch of inexplicable bile.

He went on, "It was my plan to get on in the circus. I wanted to become a higher, more important member. I suppose that I wished to be the ringleader—to be the one who bossed people about."

"That sounds . . . reasonable," Jason put in.

"Yes," Dougleglass replied, though it wasn't one-hundred-percent clear cut whether or not he had heard Jason at all. "That was my dream—a *little* dream—but that was what I wanted." He paused for a long moment. "And then I won a lottery."

"Huh?" Jason blurted out, feeling almost that this was a side-swipe.

"Yes, my wish, more than anything else was for me to make money—and for me to return to my home country."

Here Dougleglass paused, produced a handkerchief from the breast pocket of his shirt, dabbed his lips with it, and then brought out the photograph which he had showed Jason only minutes before. He gave the photograph a neat peck with his lips and then replaced it in his breast pocket. He resumed eating his meat stew, speaking to Jason from the corner of his mouth.

"Yes, he continued, "I entered a town competition—I did not understand this fully—and I was gifted with a large, cash prize, more than I could ever imagine." He gave a slack-eyed smirk. "And then fate laughed in my face."

"The elephant?" Jason asked.

" 'The elephant'," Dougleglass agreed, solemnly.

There were a few moments of silence while Dougleglass finished up his stew, apparently believing—on some level—that the subject of one's death really wasn't the sort of thing to be discussed with one's mouth full.

Jason had no complaints.

As nice as Dougleglass clearly was, Jason could quite easily have lasted a lifetime of never again seeing his yellowed and plaque-ridden teeth.

Jason had never really thought of himself as being a snob when it came to personal appearance—he was an aspiring computer programmer for God's sake!—but, he supposed that he had to draw the line somewhere.

When Dougleglass had finished up his meat stew, he again dabbed his lips with his napkin and then resumed the story which he had begun.

"Yes," Dougleglass said, "the money was a very welcome item —and something I had never quite expected to pass." He held up his hands almost as if surrendering, and then said, "But I could not exactly leave the circus alone—I did not think it right that I leave them without a juggler so soon, and, I must admit, a more pessimistic side of myself was given to believe that if— once upon a time—I managed to lose the funds then I should very much like to have not burned my bridges with the Jensen Brothers' Circus.

"And so, I decided against 'upping sticks' and blazing off into the sunset. I decided that I should do the right thing by the Anndersens, just as they had done right by me."

"And so," Jason said, "you went on with the show?"

"I went on with the show," Dougleglass agreed. "That was just how it happened. I agreed to do the shows for the next month, or until they managed to find a replacement juggler."

"But then . . ." Jason put in, already a little troubled as to just where the conversation might be headed.

"It was a normal show—I dressed up in my costume"—Dougleglass fanned his hands to indicate his lederhosen—"and I went through all the *usual* practice routines. Then, once ready to step onto the stage, I had something which I can only truly now describe as a premonition."

"A 'premonition'?"

Dougleglass nodded. "I saw *her*."

"The girl from the photo—the one you wanted to travel to go and see?"

Dougleglass shook his head. "No, it wasn't her." He shook his head again, and his complexion seemed to pale slightly, something which—in retrospect—Jason thought slightly odd for a ghost."

Dougleglass continued, "It was the lady . . . the *elderly woman*; you know the one, from the travel post."

Jason assumed that—by 'travel post'—Dougleglass meant to say the bus-station waiting room.

"Yes," Dougleglass went on, "looking back I believe that I should have read the signs, but I must admit that I had not been in so much of a sombre mood as to think death might lurk right around the corner. And yet"—here he paused and Jason heard the gentle rhythm of Dougleglass's breathing for a few moments —"it was."

Jason waited out the beats. He had been politely awaiting a blow-by-blow account of just how Dougleglass had come to bite it and he knew he wouldn't be *quite* free until he had heard Dougleglass out completely.

For a couple of moments, Dougleglass just blinked away to himself; apparently lost to a daze. And then, finally, he snapped back. "When I entered the arena, when I saw Andercheth, he looked slightly shaken. I should have seen it as a sign . . . and the . . . the . . ."

"Elephant?" Jason asked.

Dougleglass swallowed hard.

His Adam's apple bobbed up and down as if he had gone and swallowed a piece of bread whole. "Yes," he replied, "the *elephant* . . . I do not remember so well from that point onwards, but, yes, I remember the elephant, and the crushing sensation of its feet . . . knocking me to the ground . . . *trampling* me."

For a long few moments there was near silence in the kitchen tent. Only the *crackle* of flames from the stove broke the stillness.

"And then I died," Dougleglass said finally.

LIFE AFTER DEATH

To be honest, the big questions—*what/how/why*—had never much troubled Jason . . . except perhaps after he'd slogged out a marathon six-hour debugging session with no discernible outcome.

No *positive* outcome, anyway.

But now hearing it from the horse's mouth—which was to say Dougleglass's mouth—Jason realised that he was actually quite interested to hear just what happened when one 'died'.

Not that Jason let on at all.

Jason was all too aware of the emotional tenderness at stake here. He might be a programmer, but he had feelings too . . .

"So," Jason tried, "no bright lights—no singing choirs, no"— he searched his mind for other clichés—"endless abyss?"

Dougleglass remained sitting still.

Then he shook his head.

"It is impossible to explain. I cannot explain. I—at once—

existed in the Real World, but also I did not . . . do you understand that?"

Jason read Dougleglass's wrinkled brow and knew that right now he was probably better off dropping the whole issue.

"Yes," Jason said, "I completely understand."

Dougleglass gave Jason a disbelieving look—the outline of a smirk clinging on there—and then hunched his shoulders and stood. "The one thing I do know," he said, collecting up his and Jason's now-empty plates, "is that when all the world settled around me and I saw myself still on this same, *Mortal* plane, I had been relocated to the transport post."

This time, Jason couldn't help but butt in. "The bus station."

Instead of hinting at a smirk, this time Dougleglass full on *smeared* one across his lips.

"A bus-station waiting room," Jason added, already feeling that he was making a prize idiot of himself somehow.

Dougleglass's smirk only widened and, after setting their empty plates down on a counter before an unsmiling large woman dressed in a discoloured, once-white apron, he said, "Let us go outside—*to her*—because you still have so much to learn."

Jason wondered if there was—*maybe*—some option which might allow him to avoid all this 'learning'.

But, on the other hand, he didn't want to upset the apple cart.

Dougleglass guided Jason about the tents, and once more over the severely muddied ground.

Jason couldn't help wondering what might happen if he decided to scarper off somewhere.

Would Jason find himself lost in the Spiritual Past?

Or would Jason—*somehow*—reach the end of this world and pop up in his own?

Nice and returned to everyday normality . . . everyday *mundanity* . . .

. . . All right, not quite *everyday* normality seeing as he had still to do battle with Christmas Eve; not to mention the rest of the fucking festive period.

Actually, thinking about it now, how things were going, it seemed somewhat preferable to be taking the long way home for Christmas.

He would get home eventually.

The only detail was the journey itself . . .

As they walked, Dougleglass spoke to Jason over his shoulder. "That place—the transport post."

"Bus station," Jason again corrected him.

"It is the place where all the Unquiet gather; those who require another journey . . . those who had somewhere to go in their lives. It is there that the Unquiet await a Channeller—one who shall guide them on their way."

"Can't you find your way yourself?"

Dougleglass stopped walking. He turned around—dour-faced now. "No," he answered simply before treading on.

Dougleglass took them all the way up the hill which sat on the opposite side of the circus encampment. Jason could feel his whole body warming in the afternoon sunlight. It felt like it'd been almost forever since he had seen the sun.

Since Jason's usual routine was to sleep in all day and then get up around one or two in the afternoon, it meant that Jason normally got his work done at night. He had been working at night when that homeward pang had struck him. And though Jason was undoubtedly productive at night, there was the downside that he almost never got to see the sun.

This was especially compounded in winter when daylight hours were few and far between.

They worked their way up the rest of the hill and stood up there to observe the valley below.

Jason looked hard—and then he looked harder still—not quite able to believe his own eyes.

A train station.

A *steam train* pulling up.

Its smoke stack—or whatever it was called—billowing.

The scent of freshly roasting coal wafting along on the breeze.

Jason turned to look at Dougleglass, who was now beaming to himself. It was one thing to enjoy having a monopoly on information, but Jason felt that Dougleglass was taking extreme pleasure in the situation.

How *could* Dougleglass really find all this so entertaining while he was striving to get . . . wherever it was he was *striving* to get to?

It was almost masochistic in a way.

"There's no train station here," Jason said. "I mean, back in my time. The only way out of town is by bus."

Dougleglass just tapped the side of his nose knowingly and said, "Doctor Beeching, I believe, has much to answer for."

Before Jason could question just what the hell—*who the hell*—

Dougleglass was jabbering about now, Dougleglass descended the hill, headed for the train.

Once Dougleglass had bought the two of them tickets—in First Class, no less—they sat tight in their seats, sitting across from one another, and Jason couldn't help but run the gauntlet of naivety once again.

"Am I some sort of minder?"

"Hmm?" Dougleglass said, apparently a little distracted by the hillside at the stationary train's window.

" 'A minder'," Jason repeated, "you know, like somebody you employ to look after your kids—that sort of thing?"

From within his waistcoat, Dougleglass produced a brass pocket watch. Dougleglass tapped the glass twice with his finger, frowned and then replaced it from whence it came.

" 'A minder'," Dougleglass repeated back to Jason, as if he hadn't heard him the other two times. "Yes, I suppose that is one way of putting it."

There was silence for a few beats, with Dougleglass looking intently out of the window.

"What I'm getting at," Jason said, feeling struck by fresh vigour, "is what exactly is my function? Why were you stuck back at that . . .at that"—and then Jason forced himself to say it for the first time—"*transport post?*"

Dougleglass remained fixed on some spot just out the window. He seemed distracted by the train, too—almost like a commuter who wished the world would just get a move on; take him where he needed to go.

"There are certain things," Dougleglass said, "which are beyond the comprehension of any of us."

Jason wasn't having any of that, and so he shot back, "Who told *you* then?"

Dougleglass pouted slightly and then gave a shrug. "Just talk," he said.

"Talk from who?"

"Those passing through the transport post—other Unquiet, like me. Word gets around. You may call it rumour, I suppose."

Jason opened his mouth to protest some more, but, before he could do so, Dougleglass held his finger up to his lips, indicating that he should remain silent.

"If you will forgive a doddering fool, would you very much mind being quiet? It is not often we have the chance of saying goodbye to a place, let alone a past *life* . . . and that is what I precisely mean to do at this moment in time."

And, true to his word, Dougleglass did exactly that.

Then, slowly, the train slunk out of the station.

Its wheels going *clickety-clack*.

AN UNANTICIPATED TRAIN JOURNEY

J *ason fell asleep* at some point.

He wasn't quite sure when.

He found himself swept along by a series of bizarre dreams.

At first, he imagined himself as a fish . . . a fish swimming about in a tank, gliding in and out of rocks, and weed, and peering on out at the wider world—rendered as nothing more than a blur beyond the glass.

The dream shunted and shifted soon after and—all of a sudden—Jason found himself in the middle of an endless ocean; murky depths as far as his fishy eyes would allow him to see.

Jason would flounder about, following the light, seeking the way to the surface . . . but there appeared to be no way out.

He was out there, in the Big Bad World now.

Jason came to with a large *clack* of the train track beneath him.

He jerked a touch against the silky fabric of the seat.

It was disconcerting to find such a fine material used to upholster a train seat when he had grown so accustomed to the polyester—or *whatever* they were—seats used in modern times.

He could smell garlic and butter. A salty scent clung to the air of the carriage.

When he blinked, the world returned to him detail by detail.

He glanced out the window briefly, saw that it was night, and then noticed the reflection in the glass. He could see a woman, wearing the train line uniform, waiting patiently with a ticket puncher.

The ticket inspector.

Jason glanced across to Dougleglass and saw that—*already*—he was handing their tickets over. When Dougleglass had bought the tickets, Jason couldn't recall.

As the inspector passed the tickets back to Dougleglass, and then made to leave their compartment, she took a good eyeful of Jason.

When the door to the compartment slid shut, Dougleglass leaned across to Jason in a conspiratorial manner, and said, "It is the way you are dressed."

Jason, almost having forgotten he was wearing clothes at all, took stock of his dress. He concurred that; yes, hoodie and jeans *did* seem somewhat out of place in this context . . . whichever context *this* exactly was.

"I was thinking," Dougleglass said, "that we should, perhaps, relocate to the dining car."

As the wafting scent of the garlic and butter returned to Jason's nostrils, all he could think to do was nod in reply.

The First Class dining car was really all that Jason might've expected.

It consisted of several—*quaint-looking*—round tables, covered in white table cloths; each with its own personal gas lamp.

Dougleglass led Jason over to one of the tables toward the back of the carriage, and, as Jason sat down, he took stock of the people around him.

This was obviously peak dining time and Jason found himself surrounded by elegant travelling men and women—dressed in their formal best.

Jason noted, at the same time, that while he was hardly setting the world alight with his choice of outfit then so neither was Dougleglass in his lederhosen with the neat white shirt underneath.

Although, to be fair, it was obvious which one of the two of them stood out the most.

And it wasn't Dougleglass.

At least, to eat, Dougleglass had shucked the traditional Bavarian hat he'd been wearing . . . that hat *was* from Bavaria, wasn't it?

A waiter soon arrived to the table and took their orders, with Dougleglass insisting that they go for nothing less than a full seven-course meal.

Jason was somewhat taken aback by this show of opulence— and apparently the waiter was too, judging by his arched eyebrow. Once the waiter had disappeared off, Dougleglass leaned over the table and remarked, "Can't a fellow enjoy the last journey of his life if he wishes?"

Jason had nothing to say to that so he just kept his lips sealed.

When their food arrived, Jason was pleasantly surprised to find himself facing off with a bowl of leak-and-potato soup, and he dug into it with great vigour. The wheaty bread—all warmed up so that it near enough melted in his mouth—was another great victory.

Being a vegetarian, Jason wasn't convinced that he would find anything further in the meal satisfactory . . . but he was so very wrong.

The warming leak-and-potato soup was followed by a plate of mussels; all of them smeared in the aforementioned garlic and butter; and although Jason had always been greatly suspect of any sort of sea food—and its impact upon his vegetarian status— he couldn't quite see himself passing up the opportunity right now.

And he was extremely glad that he *didn't* pass it up.

The mussels seemed to melt at the back of his throat, warming him on their way down.

Jason was a little shocked when Dougleglass decided to order a great, big bubbly bottle of champagne, the cork of which Jason sent pinging up into the ceiling.

And although Jason was a teetotalitarian, he did have a few sips of his flute.

They got through with dinner without so much as a word to one another; not that Jason minded all that much. He was some-what preoccupied with all the delicious food which kept arriving in front of him in an endless barrage.

When they did get through with dessert—chocolate fondue

—Jason sipped on his cup of black coffee and wondered whether he would ever be able to stand up again.

As it turned out, he didn't need to know the answer to that question right away, because another came tumbling right out from between his lips. "So," Jason said, setting his coffee cup back down on the table, "Who *is* this girl?"

Dougleglass stayed quiet for several moments, staring into the blackness of his coffee.

For some reason, Jason wondered if—*perhaps*—Dougleglass was imagining that the coffee within his cup might represent some sort of an abyss.

But, before Jason had the chance to enquire further—had he been so inclined—Dougleglass replied.

"She was my One True Love," Dougleglass said, and the gentlest of smiles traced his lips.

Jason felt a slight tightening in his gut at hearing *those* words emanating from Dougleglass's lips, but he tried not to give too much away.

Something about 'love' didn't sit right with him.

Was it the fact that it was an intangible?

Something which could never *quite* be debugged completely from the lines upon lines of code which formed the human mind?

. . . Something like that . . .

Dougleglass remained silent for a few seconds as if he —*himself*—was reverent to Jason's own thoughts, and then he said, "We both agreed, in the small town where we lived, that there were not any of the opportunities which we might find elsewhere." He paused here, Jason thought because he might be tearing up, but—in the end—Dougleglass only slugged back another dose of coffee and went on.

"Although my love was a seamstress, and could find work within the town, there was nothing there for me . . . nothing which would be substantial enough to allow us to fulfil our dreams."

In his slightly inebriated state, Jason thought of breaking in with a question—out of politeness more than anything else—but he instead opted to withhold his counsel.

"And so, it was decided that I should go out into the world and find my fortune—*oh*, we were *engaged*, of course, that was something which we could not put off even if the marriage itself would need to be postponed for the time being."

"So," Jason said, "When you came into money, from the lottery, you'd managed to find your fortune? Then you were required to return to her?"

Dougleglass smiled. "Not 'required', young man, but, yes, the plan was for me to return to my village, to make my true love my wife."

There was a drawn-out silence between Jason and Dougleglass at the table, and it was only then that Jason realised that—for the most part—the dining cart had emptied of other passengers.

Dougleglass and Jason were alone.

This time, it was Jason who broke the silence.

"What was her name?" Jason said.

Dougleglass continued to stare down into his emptied cup of coffee, apparently examining the grains—could he tell a fortune from coffee grounds, or was that mumbo-jumbo only possible with tea leaves?

Jason had to admit that he had never been sufficiently mind-numbingly bored to ever contemplate the matter.

"Elsa," Dougleglass replied, finally. "Elsa was her name."

ARRIVAL ... OF A KIND

The *train barrelled on* through the night and Jason had to admit to being somewhat glad for the sturdy heating on board. And also for the blanket which one of the attendants had given him.

The blanket was a burgundy shade—woolly, but *not* wool . . . Jason could tell because otherwise he would've come out in a red rash within moments of touching it.

Also, rather than the constant movement of the carriage making Jason nauseous, it actually lulled him into a deep and smooth sleep.

Thankfully, though, there was no more of those slightly odd fish-in-a-tank dream sequences.

When Jason felt the train gently slowing, he woke.

He shifted open an eyelid and gazed out, realising that—in the night—the whole terrain had up and changed on him.

Whereas before there'd been rolling green hills and merry,

flat, wide-open spaces; Jason now found himself confronted by huge snow-capped mountain peaks, and a rushing river, alongside the railway tracks.

When he turned to look at Dougleglass, who was peering out through the window, Jason could only think to say, "But the Channel Tunnel hasn't been built yet . . . there's no way to go between the British Isles and mainland Europe by train . . . not for, what, a hundred years?"

That comment came on the tails of knowledge long-ago engraved in his brain.

It was something which every British schoolchild knew . . . the only means for accessing mainland Europe by land was through the Channel Tunnel.

Yes siree, the very British solution of, all at once, laying out the invitation for the continent to come and visit, via the railway tunnel, while still holding up a staunch—and not to mention *unambiguous*—hand to prevent foreigners from getting *too close*.

A *bridge* would've been out of the question.

And, engineering issues aside; it would've been *exceptionally* vulgar.

Jason looked to Dougleglass, expecting to have—*for once*—boxed him into a very tight, and uncomfortable, corner. But there was *that* smirk again.

And Jason surely knew what was coming next.

"That is magic for you," Dougleglass said.

"What?" Jason replied, a snap to his voice.

He supposed that the champagne from last night was still coursing about his veins . . . he wondered if this First Class carriage might provide complimentary Alka-Seltzer.

"The train flew"—and here Dougleglass illustrated the point by fluttering his fingertips—"all while you were sleeping."

Jason's mouth latched open wide.

So many questions of logic.

So much which just didn't make *any* sense.

. . . But where to begin?

And, sensing impending defeat, Jason decided to just give over.

The explanation was what it was . . . *an* explanation.

Dougleglass examined his pocket watch once again, and then peered over the top of the brass casing at him. "Are you ready to continue on our journey?"

Jason checked in with himself.

And realised he had little choice.

The station bustled with activity, and any sort of suspicion which might've still clung to Jason's mind that they might —*somehow*—still be in England was soon lost.

And Jason without his passport!

He really *had* managed to allow this stranger to take full advantage of him.

. . . Albeit a stranger who had paid his way, and fed him well . . . and then there was the fact that the stranger was a ghost; or an *Unquiet*, as seemed to be the politically correct definition.

Jason allowed these concerns to drift to the fringes of his mind, and he took in the people dashing about the crowd— briefcases and umbrellas, and all else poking out as they went on their way.

What struck Jason the most was how seemingly everybody wore a hat.

Men and women.

Young and old.

If he'd spotted a cat or a dog, travelling with his owner, he wouldn't have been surprised to see them *also* wearing a hat.

He eyed the signs about the station and saw that they were all painted in rather regal greens with golden lettering. Every couple of minutes another train rolled into the station with a cacophony of screeching brakes and endless plumes of steam.

Jason breathed in the copper-tasting steam, and, at the same time as he had the flavour of copper on his tongue, he tasted the thick *pipe* smoke of a passer-by.

Jason spluttered a couple of times—never really ever having had the most resilient airways in the world—and then he searched for Dougleglass, who was striding on off.

In maybe a couple of moments' time, Dougleglass would've become lost among the rest of the commuters.

Jason hustled on through the crowds, really trying hard to keep his wits about him. He felt the warm materials, the fine threads of his fellow travellers' clothing, and he couldn't help but feel a slight, pleasant throb at the base of his gut. There was something about an adventure, this sensation he couldn't quite describe, which sent a tingle through his blood, and seemed to cause his heart to skip a few beats faster than usual.

Or maybe Jason was just on the brink of having a panic attack . . . that could be it too.

Quite easily.

Before Jason got too carried away by his neuroses, Dougle-glass grabbed a hold of the front of his sweatshirt.

Through gnashed teeth, and with an expression which, for the first time, was anything else but a sort of arrogant sense of superiority, he said, "Come on, we are in a hurry!"

Jason found himself being hustled along, between the travellers and toward—he assumed—the exit to the street.

If Jason had been forced at gunpoint into describing the street outside the station, he might've settled on a description along the lines of 'alpine'.

Underfoot there were cobblestones, and there was a scent of long grasses, and roast pork blowing on the wind. It was a touch chillier up here than it had been back at the circus tent; and this despite the fact it was, apparently, summer.

When the sun came out from behind a cloud, however, Jason felt waves of warmth passing through his cheeks, burrowing deep into his blood . . . until the familiar mountain chill returned and rendered the previous feeling—for the most part—somewhat redundant.

Dougleglass continued to hurry Jason along, and Jason couldn't help but observe the wrinkles of strain which had emerged on Dougleglass's brow.

Jason wished there was something he could do or say to set things right, but he had never been good at any of that off-the-cuff thinking, when it came to human-human interaction.

He had never had the chance to get the knack of it, what with all the staring at a screen he did.

And so they hurried onward, up the steep slope which Jason imagined led out of the quaint little town. It was only when they reached a narrow little road which curled its way about the mountain that Dougleglass snatched a look at his pocket watch.

Halted.

Then said, in an exasperated voice, "Time has run out. I cannot reach her."

And—just like that—the whole world appeared to dissolve about Jason.

Blackness leaked into everything.

OUT OF TIME

F or some reason, Jason imagined he would return to the bus-station waiting room—or the 'transport post', as Dougle-glass had phrased it.

But, no.

What actually happened was that Jason found himself in a dark space—he might have called it an *abyss*—where he was confronted, standing almost nose-to-nose with the elderly woman in the duffel coat.

The one who had stopped time.

The lady's eyes were wide, and her lips were slightly parted. When she spoke, her words didn't come as sound waves through Jason's ears—they passed directly into Jason's mind . . . fully formed thoughts and feelings, but ones which, Jason knew, were not his own.

— *Channeller. It is your responsibility. The weight falls upon you. The burden is your own.*

Jason supposed that 'Channeller' did indeed refer to himself. He had to admit that—in the past; in his past experience—he had always been somewhat disappointed that psychics, or whatever, always seemed to need to ask people's names . . . rather than *divine* them.

But, perhaps, the old woman didn't *need* Jason's name right now . . . or maybe she was stowing that particular card away for later.

When she needed to show off some skills.

Or maybe instil some fear . . .

Something like that.

Jason found himself losing his mind to the pale blue eyes of the old woman, and, more than anything, he longed to be back in that alpine village; with Dougleglass . . . even though Dougleglass had been in a bad mood . . .

Jason was readying himself to soak up some more knowledge from the elderly woman, but, apparently, this seemed all she had planned for him.

She slipped back, motionlessly, into the lurking shadows of the abyss and the world—or whatever this 'Spiritual Past' constituted—bled back into being.

Or what *passed* for being.

Jason blinked away his daze and then realised, out of the corner of his eye, that Dougleglass had taken off striding along the small twirling mountain roadway.

Jason pursued him.

Caught up with him.

Managed to match his pace and—*somehow*—interrogate him.

"What happened?" Jason said. "What were we late for—how did time run out?"

Dougleglass gave a shake of his head and buttoned his lip; now striding along with increased vigour.

"Where're you going now?" Jason said.

When Dougleglass spoke this time, his accent was much stronger, as his second language appeared to escape him. "How you say? I am *off* to go and kill myself."

"I . . . I . . ." Jason managed to get out, between respirations. "It's just—I thought . . . you're already . . . you know?"

Dougleglass stopped his personally enforced march. He stood square-shouldered and stared Jason between the eyes. "Because I am already *dead?*"

"Well, yeah," Jason said.

That remark earned Jason another of Dougleglass's now famous smirks. "There is still a lot for a Channeller like yourself to learn."

Dougleglass continued on his way, apparently not too bothered by Jason's presence.

"All right," Jason said, "then how about you explain to me, in simple-to-understand terms, just why you're going to kill yourself?"

Dougleglass kept up his smile. "Because," he said, "there's no *point* anymore."

Jason realised that this whole conversation was going to be one long ascension before Dougleglass finally gave out what he meant. "And why was there no point anymore?"

Dougleglass remained silent, still striding onward. "We missed the last carriage—the one which would've carried us to my village."

"But don't you have the lottery money—the money which you won back in England?"

Dougleglass shook his head. His wry smile at his superior knowledge all but vanished and he stomped onward. "Nobody here would accept that money."

"How'd you know?" Jason said.

"Just believe me with this one—it is *my* country, after all."

The two of them carried on—both headed toward their apparent doom.

At least in the Spiritual Past.

Jason racked his brains.

He tried to hit upon an explanation but none at all seemed forthcoming. He still felt somewhat disorientated. He couldn't quite piece his mind back together.

And then, in a field which sat alongside the mountain road, Jason spied a pair of horses.

Though Jason was a long way from being an expert on horses, he could tell that there was a brown one and a white one.

Both of them tore at verdant tufts of grass sprouting on the other side of the fence.

Jason glanced forward, realised that Dougleglass had got himself a good twenty, or thirty, paces clear and would—no doubt—go through with his wishes if left to his own devices. Jason called out to Dougleglass, fully expecting to be ignored.

But Dougleglass did turn his head.

Jason held still.

The two of them exchanged glances for the longest time.

Then Jason said, "I've got an idea."

TIME TO BELIEVE

T en *minutes later*—although to the law-abiding and deeply
karma-obeying Jason it felt much, much longer—the two
of them stampeded along on the backs of the purloined horses.

Jason had never been one to take up horse-riding so he was
having severe difficulty in keeping himself atop the white horse
he'd picked out for himself and—all things considered—was glad
to have Dougleglass riding along on the brown one beside him.

Occasionally, Dougleglass would reach out and take hold of
Jason's horse's mane and speak quiet German words into its ear
whenever it appeared to be getting out of control . . . which—to
Jason—seemed to be happening *all* the time . . .

Then again, Jason had always believed that if there had
existed a Richter scale for wimps then he would've ranked very
highly indeed.

As they pounded along the mountain road, and Jason found
himself feeling a touch—*only a touch*—more sure of this horse-

riding business, he called out, "Is this better than killing yourself?"

Dougleglass either didn't hear, or the smirk in profile was his answer.

They rode onward for what seemed like hours, but which—in reality—could've been as short as twenty minutes.

That was the thing about the Real World. Jason found that time seemed to move one *hell* of a lot slower than when you were slumped in front of a computer screen.

Finally, after passing through many a field and over—*to Jason's extreme despair*—many a *fence*, they emerged on what appeared to be a quiet back lane. Jason glanced about himself, somehow sensing that they were nearing their destination.

Or maybe Jason was just delusional.

It seemed as if he had been in Dougleglass's company for a lifetime . . . although, then again, a lifetime could last over a hundred years; or be as short and decisive as a single heartbeat.

Dougleglass rode his horse, gently clicking his tongue; urging it onward with gentle squeezes of his heels. Soon enough, Jason found the two of them stood before a dainty little wooden-beamed cottage.

Jason looked the place over.

He took in the white-washed picket fence and, just beyond, the prim garden, clearly kept in check by a pair of female-wielded secateurs . . . which wasn't to say that Jason believed a woman's place was in a garden, or even in a kitchen, for that matter.

In actual fact, Jason couldn't confidently say just where any sort of woman—real or theoretical—was supposed to be.

To say that women were a mystery to Jason was putting it mildly.

Very mildly indeed . . .

Dougleglass stopped before the garden gate. All of a sudden, he seemed quite hesitant, like he wasn't sure what to do next.

Cottoning onto his role as Channeller, Jason decided this was the sort of thing he was supposed to help Unquiet souls out with.

"Uh," Jason began, unconvincingly.

Dougleglass turned to look at Jason—his expression now totally neutral. He might've been feeling afraid, he could've felt angry, or desperate, Jason really had no way of knowing.

There just wasn't sufficient output for Jason to be one-hundred per cent sure.

Jason realised that he *had* to say something now that he had raised his voice. "Why don't you, you know—"

And then Jason made a vague shunting gesture, in the direction of the front door of the cottage.

Dougleglass stood firm, on the back of his horse.

Jason wondered if it was because of the over-powering scent of his own horse that he felt the thick, unruly odour of the roses in the garden so sensitively in his nostrils.

He could almost catch the tangy scent on his tongue and right at the back of his throat.

In the near distance, he heard the sound of something stirring, but—when he turned to look—he saw it was only the wind.

He turned back to Dougleglass, feeling a slight, twisting sensation deep in his gut.

No matter how hard Jason attempted to ignore the sensation, it was impossible.

Something from somewhere—from some *time*—had a hold over him.

What it was, Jason couldn't say.

Another of those *damn* intangibles.

Dougleglass remained sat upright on his horse, apparently immovable.

And then he spoke, in slightly drawling tones. "This doesn't *feel* right," he said, and then shifted a sidelong glance in Jason's direction. "Just doesn't *feel* real; that's all."

Jason really didn't want to get into his whole "What is real?" debate in the Spiritual Past, so he just gave an understanding nod.

Or he hoped it *looked* understanding.

"I've wanted this," Dougleglass went on, "for such a long time, and now that it is here, now that I have got what I wanted, I'm afraid to believe."

Despite the somewhat emotionally stormy setting, Jason couldn't help thinking to himself that Dougleglass wasn't so smug now . . . no more of that self-assured smirking business.

But even through that—*slightly tainted*—feeling of relief at their improved interpersonal relations, Jason felt the words passing through him.

What he needed to say right now.

And so he said it.

"Time to believe."

A LONG TIME COMING

D ougleglass *remained still* for several long moments.
No emotion crossed his features.

For some reason, Jason considered that the elderly woman in the duffel coat might've—*somehow*—managed to freeze time here, in the Spiritual Past . . . and why Jason saw that as being something of a great feat really riled him in a way he had been previously unable to imagine . . . but why?

What would be her motive?

Why this very moment?

Why *right* now?

But—as Jason soon witnessed—time wasn't frozen at all.

On the contrary, it was very much moving along just like normal.

Dougleglass's expression seemed to at last find focus. His previously, deeply ingrained wrinkles in his forehead unkneaded themselves. His tightly held lips unwound to produce a gleaming smile.

A *gleaming* smile which Jason never would have believed Dougleglass able to produce if he hadn't been witnessing it for himself.

Maybe it was something about Jason which meant Dougleglass didn't do much smiling around him, or—perhaps more likely—Dougleglass was weighed down by the responsibility of seeing out the final stages of his 'life'.

Yes, that, quite possibly, might also explain his sombre mood.

But Dougleglass was smiling now.

That was the main thing.

Dougleglass shifted from one foot to the other and Jason stood apart from him, already trying to imagine himself in Dougleglass's lederhosen and knee-high boots.

That Bavarian hat perched on his head.

Was Dougleglass trembling slightly?

Jason couldn't quite be one-hundred-per-cent sure.

Dougleglass reached out for the brass knocker fastened to the cherry-red painted front door. He slipped Jason a sidelong glance, gave him a subtle—almost unnoticeable—nod, and then brought the knocker down three times.

Rap. Rap. Rap.

Jason's heart stuck in his throat for long—*achingly long*—seconds. He began to wonder if he'd become stuck in time once more, and it was only when he stood by and observed the front door open in on itself, and an attractive, young blond girl; wearing a sapphire-blue dress; her hair arranged in ringlets; that Jason felt his body spring back into motion.

Dougleglass lost all recollection of Jason's presence as he was drawn into the blond girl.

Jason observed the two of them embrace.

He looked over the façade of the house; to the holly wreaths and to the candles which decorated the tiny, potted Christmas tree standing beside the front door. He felt a couple of flakes of snow flutter down and brush against his cheeks.

But they didn't chill him.

They *warmed* him.

From the inside.

Jason felt like something of a voyeur here. He felt distinctly uncomfortable about the fact that he might be *somehow* 'intruding' on this precious, intimate, moment between long-lost lovers.

Jason took a couple of steps back.

He turned away from the cottage—half-thinking of the horses, and how he could probably just about manage to ride himself back to the village where they had come from.

But, as Jason attempted to slip away undetected, Dougleglass called out after him.

"Jason!" Dougleglass said. "Where do you think you are going?"

Jason held himself still; now a touch panicked because, as a new Channeller, he really had little—*no*—grasp of the etiquette. Of the etiquette which detailed how a Channeller should act once they'd '*channelled*' their Unquiet.

Without etiquette, Jason was lost.

Completely.

No rules, for Jason, meant that there was no *order* either . . . and such a world was—*quite simply*—unimaginable.

So Jason tried not to imagine it.

Dougleglass's eyes now danced in such a way that Jason never would've believed to be possible.

It was almost like he had a whole bundle of energy bouncing around within him.

"Please," Dougleglass said, "you come inside, with us?"

Jason looked to the pretty blond girl, to the woman who Jason had—*apparently*—brought Dougleglass to, and he couldn't help feeling a slight *fizzle* about his veins.

Jason had done this.

He had brought the two of them together.

. . . Oh, sure, he'd had some help with directions; but Dougleglass himself had claimed that only a Channeller could aid the Unquiet's travels into the past.

The knowledge that he'd done *something* good was almost too much for him to fathom.

As Jason took a step toward Dougleglass, and the woman he held in his arms, he felt the ground shifting from out beneath his feet.

And—just like that—everything was gone.

Darkness crept up upon Jason once more.

LACKING

The backs of Jason's eyelids burned fire-red.

He could feel himself spinning around at a great speed.

He reached out for something to hold onto, but found nothing at all. He wondered if he would ever stop moving . . . and it was at that precise moment that Jason realised he *had*.

Jason's feet were firmly grounded and—as if from the tinniest of speakers, and with the lowest amount of volume—he realised he could hear Christmas music.

Jingling bells.

An upbeat melody.

Yes, it was Christmas music all right.

Jason switched his mind back to his surroundings.

He opened his eyes.

Beige-toned walls.

Strip lighting.

Those odd-looking strangers.

The old woman in the duffel coat.

And that girl . . . the one he had noticed before. Still wearing those wrap-around headphones, off in a world of her own.

It was then that Jason recalled just what Dougleglass had said to him. All that he had explained. That everybody here, in this waiting room, was dead.

For some reason, Jason caught a whiff of something antibacterial in his nostrils. It sent shivers right down to his bones. Made it almost seem as if his blood itself might be humming.

It seemed to dull all taste—all sensation—that might've occupied his mouth.

On instinct, Jason turned to look over in the corner of the bus-station waiting room.

The elderly woman in the duffel coat was sitting upright . . . and she was staring right at him.

Jason glanced about.

He realised he was standing at the sliding doors; that it was as if he had simply reappeared *here*, inside the waiting room, after only going outside for a quick walk around the block.

What was Jason supposed to do now?

Should he just leave?

Head out of the waiting room?

Surely now, Jason's bus must've arrived . . . he *had* been to an entirely different country, after all.

But when Jason glanced back to the departures screen, expecting to see all the normal listings of buses soon to leave, there was nothing.

Nothing but a blank screen.

Acting on instinct, Jason glanced over to the elderly woman in the duffel coat.

She continued to stare back at him.

Jason wondered if he should go over.

If she was *inviting* him over.

Jason unplugged himself from his spot by the doors and trod over to where his bag, and the elderly woman, awaited him.

The elderly woman did not smile, or take her eyes off him—continuing to glare away—and Jason felt almost as if he was drawn to her.

He sat down on the bench beside her.

They remained in silence for several seconds, and then, without so much as moving her lips, the woman spoke to Jason.

Spoke into his mind.

— What're you looking for, Channeller?

Somewhat uninitiated in all this Channeller business, Jason replied out loud.

"I'm sorry?" he said.

There was a brief pause and then the old woman spoke into Jason's mind once more.

— What do you lack?

Jason pondered this a moment.

He couldn't help but think that the question was somewhat obscure. He wondered if the old lady might be enquiring—in some roundabout way—if he was hungry.

Or thirsty.

The old woman, however, before Jason could so much as sow the *seed* of an answer, was speaking again:

— Those who are, or who become, Channellers, it is because, shall we say, they lack a certain something in their lives. There is a specific absence

75

which seems to attract such supernatural powers. And, allow me to assure you, Jason, your powers are really quite supernatural indeed.

There was that party trick he'd been waiting for.

She knew his name without him having to tell her.

Then again, should he have really been all that surprised when she apparently had no difficulty in speaking directly into his mind?

It took Jason a couple of moments to get his head around just what it was she was implying . . . implying *no*, because she was straight out saying exactly what she thought in words.

Luckily for Jason, there was little-to-no interpretation required.

"I . . ." Jason began, "when you say that I lack something in my own life; that I have these especially potent powers, I have to admit that I don't really follow you . . . not really *at all*."

There was another lengthy silence, and Jason realised that all the others; the lady with the feather boa, the guy dressed in a chicken suit, and the attractive girl his own age; were all staring right at him.

And why *shouldn't* they?

He was jabbering on at the elderly woman in the duffel coat when she hadn't so much as spoken a word to him.

Not *out loud*, in any case.

The elderly woman in the duffel coat spoke to Jason again:

— *Channeller, even for one such as yourself, it's really better not to speak out loud. Not even to the dead.*

And then she tapped her temple as if to indicate madness.

Somehow, Jason felt that he had heard this—or something like it—before.

— *Look around you, Channeller.*

Jason, assuming that the old woman in the duffel coat could really only be talking to one person—*him*—did as she requested.

The others, the Unquiet—*the dead*—had all returned to their personal waiting rituals; apparently no longer interested in paying attention to him.

The guy in the chicken suit sat with his hands hunching his knees back into his chest, rocking ever so slightly.

Meanwhile, the lady in the feather boa was examining her immaculately painted crimson fingernails.

The girl about the same age as Jason was lightly bobbing her head in time to the music playing in her headphones.

Jason could smell the disinfectant coming back to him, and the wooden bench which he sat upon felt hard against his backside. It creaked when he shifted his weight ever-so slightly, attempting to get more comfortable. His mouth felt a little numb and he could taste a morsel of the onion-and-lentil soup he'd chugged down before leaving his halls of residence . . . what he wouldn't have given for a hot cup of soup right now.

That would *really* do the trick.

Was it his imagination or had the temperature in the waiting room dropped a couple of degrees in the past few minutes?

As if expecting an explanation, Jason looked over to the old woman in the duffel coat; but she remained impossibly still. Her dead-eyed stare intercepted his.

Jason wondered what was coming next.

He had done what she'd asked of him.

He'd *looked around . . .* now what?

— *Most Channellers, they help only one, and they learn something about themselves, but—tonight—I do believe that Christmas Eve offers an extra-special, wonderful opportunity. A time for giving.*

" 'A time for giving'?" Jason repeated at her.

It was only as the words tumbled out past his lips that he recalled what the old woman had said about *not* speaking out loud . . . not even in the presence of the Unquiet.

In the presence of dead people.

The elderly woman went on:

— *Yes, 'a time for giving'. Call it my little gift to you . . . a* Christmas *gift; if you like.*

Jason wasn't quite sure *what* he could call all of this—what he'd *like* to call all of this—and so he settled on leaving it untitled for now.

Somehow leaving this whole sorry episode untitled seemed to make it less real . . . or so he hoped.

But it was then that he noticed the *lady* in the feather boa rise up off her seat and make for the sliding doors of the bus-station waiting room.

Jason, more out of hope than expectation, cast a glance in the direction of the flat-screen monitor which—*allegedly*—would show the bus departure times . . . but, no, nothing.

What had he *expected?*

And so, Jason set off after the lady in the feather boa.

Back out into the night.

As Jason slipped out through the doors, he heard the elderly woman in the duffel coat speak to him once more:

— *Good luck.*

AROUND AGAIN

As *Jason headed back outside*, into the cool night air, his mind continued to swirl with all the consternation about just what the old woman in the duffel coat had been getting at.

Where had she got off in saying that he 'lacked' something in his life?

To begin with, Jason hadn't got much started with his life yet.

He had just about got his head around university—around the concept that, as long as he studied long and hard; a comfortable life would be awaiting him.

And that was what he wanted . . . wasn't it?

So how the old woman had suggested that he was 'lacking' something really did seem somewhat premature.

But, then again, she possessed the ability to speak into his mind. So might not she be somebody worth listening to?

Or, perhaps, Jason was just going crazy.

That was certainly a logical possibility.

As Jason walked along the street, he eyed the lady in the feather boa, and couldn't help envying her fur jacket—was it mink? No matter what his views on the ethical treatment of animals might've been, it looked warm.

Jason certainly had misjudged the temperature for this *particular* Christmas Eve because his hoodie was hardly sufficient for keeping out the cold.

Although Jason had come through one of these 'encounters' already, he couldn't help but wonder just how he should go about approaching this woman in her feather boa.

He knew nothing about her. But, then again, he had known nothing about Dougleglass either . . . and that hadn't stopped them from getting along fine, for the most part . . .

So Jason just supposed he should go for it.

He glanced at the woman—in profile—trying to judge something—*anything*—which might prompt a conversation. In the end, however, he settled on, the slightly sleazy, "I'll be your Channeller for the evening."

The woman in the feather boa did not turn to look at Jason and he was—all at once—certain that he had just committed some abhorrent *faux pas*. It froze Jason up. As he felt himself freeze up, he followed her gaze, along what had once been the bustling main street of the town, but which was now only a dirt track—mud all stirred up by horses' hoofs; deep puddles formed in the rutted pits created by carriage wheels.

There was nothing here now.

Not even the cottages like there had been when Jason had travelled back with Dougleglass . . . not so much as a single human-manipulated light source.

Only the moon.

And the hills.

Sweeping back away from them.

Slowly, taking her time, the woman in the feather boa turned to face him.

Jason read the leathered wrinkles gathered about her eyes, ingrained in her forehead. A gentle scent of lavender clung to her; a fragrance which Jason could not shake from his mind as being inextricably tied to the lavatory, and to his grandmother.

In his university halls, the cleaners always used some substance or other which smelled of lavender.

Still, despite drawing that particular parallel, it shook nothing of the woman's elegance, of what Jason was sure he'd read about—in those dreadful books he'd been compelled to study in English back at school—as being 'good breeding'.

A higher class.

Or a class higher than Jason was accustomed to, anyway.

She frowned lightly at Jason, and then she parted her lips.

Although Jason could tell the woman was committing some effort in keeping her glare cold—*pointed*—he couldn't fail to notice a certain *sparkle* which danced out from beyond the glassy surface of her eyes.

"Good evening," she said, her voice—as Jason suspected—striking a higher register than Jason's own.

Jason smiled warmly back at her, and she did her best to reciprocate, but Jason could see—almost right away—that she was clearly *not* the smiling type.

She nodded off in the direction of the trail—of the well-trodden path they stood on. "I never thought it would end as it did." Her tone was dry, detached, and Jason could tell—without asking—that she had been waiting an awfully long time for somebody to take her home.

But Jason could only listen to her.

Pay attention to what she had to say.

"A highway man," she said, arching an eyebrow, then pointing back off along the road which sat before them. "Back there. He stopped the coach, took our jewellery and a cash delivery before shooting all of us—the driver and the horses included—as if it were the most natural thing in the whole *damn* world."

That 'damn' jarred with Jason.

He knew that a lady of her 'stock' would not have dared speak like that among her own society.

Among her equals.

Trying to think of something to say in this rather poor excuse for a conversation, Jason blurted out, "Um, where're you headed?"

The lady didn't respond to Jason right away, and Jason was convinced she was—once more—lost in her own world, far from here. But then she nodded out ahead and murmured, "Our carriage is here."

And, sure enough, it was.

Jason took in the carriage. Its baby-blue painted exterior. Already he was certain he could feel the warmth from inside, beckoning him in.

A pair of horses breathed thick exhalations into the frosty, night-time air. As far as Jason could tell—only by moonlight— the horses were both black. Well-muscled beasts. They were harnessed tightly with, what appeared to Jason, to be slickly smooth restraints. The carriage itself looked somewhat roomy—roomy enough to accommodate both Jason and the lady without too much trouble, anyway.

Before Jason could really get a handle on what was going on, the lady stuck her hand out at Jason, and Jason—not really understanding what this meant, but finally catching a clue—helped her up the step and into the carriage.

Jason strode along on the well-rutted track, still all mucky beneath his feet. He really, truly knew nothing about what to expect.

But, then again, did it really matter?

Though Jason hadn't ever much thought about it before, he was somewhat surprised to find the trip in the carriage uncomfortable. He spent the entire time jerking backward and forward; never able to fully remain in one position. In the end, he settled for lying snug up against the velvet cushions which lined the carriage and staring on out through the too-thin, icicle-cold glass into the countryside *soaked* in black. The glass rattled in the windowpanes.

They'd been riding for many minutes when Jason heard the lady speak up.

In fact, it wasn't her voice that he noticed first, but her gloved hand outstretched toward him.

"Lady Gweniveere," she said, smartly.

Feeling somewhat taken aback, Jason shook her limp grip and was quite glad to be able to *not* touch her any longer.

It was almost like she transmitted some sort of freeze ray.

Right through him.

Cut him down to the bone.

When Jason breathed in now, he—somehow—breathed in cinnamon, whether it was the lady's perfume, or some sort of a scent which'd been sprayed liberally about the carriage, he couldn't really tell.

"I do apologise," Lady Gweniveere said in a tone which implied the exact opposite, "but one is certainly *not* accustomed to being, ah, to *sharing* such intimate details of one's life with a stranger." She adjusted her glove slightly, and then, in profile, arched an eyebrow. "But the world is not much of an *appropriate* place, is it?"

It caught Jason off guard when Lady Gweniveere fired a severe glare at him, as if daring him to challenge what she said.

So Jason did the only thing he believed 'appropriate', he answered, "Yes, ma'am."

Lady Gweniveere let out a long-held sigh. She examined her gloved hands some more as if she had discovered a piece of lint, or—heaven *forbid*—a tear.

She widened her eyes but aside from that she did not recognise Jason. It was almost as if Lady Gweniveere was communing with some kind of a spirit . . .

For all Jason knew, she was.

"My first marriage," she continued, "was such a tragedy—just one long depression followed by the next." She reached up to brush a lock of grey hair away from her eye—it had come out of place because of the rocking motion of the carriage—and then she continued, "It was arranged, or as 'arranged' as might've been expected. My father, you see, he was a Navy man and he never could stand the prospect of me doing whatever I might wish." This time she did look Jason directly in the eye. "A most serious man."

"I can imagine," Jason said, although he really couldn't.

Lady Gweniveere rolled her eyes upward and Jason wondered if she might comment on his status of 'silent partner' in this particular conversation. But she continued unabated.

"My father prearranged a meeting with one of his Navy acquaintances, a—by all means of appearance—career man who had stopped at nothing in becoming Rear Admiral, and who, it was believed, had been earmarked for a bright future in politics." She batted a bored eyelid. "I never did pay much attention to all those droning conversations in smoky rooms."

Jason thought that if he himself had been alive in Lady Gweniveere's times then he would've had a somewhat similar reaction to being put through such situations . . . but—then again—he didn't necessarily believe that he would've been 'privileged' enough to be present in such noble company. There were surely no computer programmers in Lady Gweniveere's times so —most likely—the closest Jason would've got to such a situation was cleaning out the toilets, or being tried as a witch for his no-holds-barred logical thinking.

Lady Gweniveere was glancing out through the blackened glass, into the night-time countryside.

For just a second, Jason thought he noticed a quiver of her lip . . . but he might've been mistaken because when she turned back to look at him she was deadly serious.

Her expression was devoid of any emotion at all.

Jason speculated that Lady Gweniveere would've been an absolute master at poker . . . poker in the flesh, that was, if she'd been playing online all the blankness of expression would've counted for precisely *zilch*.

"Still," Lady Gweniveere went on, "being tiresome perhaps wasn't the most solidly founded reason for his murder."

Jason's ears pricked up.

His blood ran cold.

Was she saying what he *thought* she was saying?

MURDER

A most uncomfortable silence followed.
And it seemed Lady Gweniveere had no intention of being the one to break it.

The carriage trundled on along the rutted road, and Jason busied himself with his attempts to stay somewhat still. He was —for the most part—*un*successful.

He felt the rub of the velvet cloth up against his arm, and he could smell a slight tang of horse manure in the air now. Perhaps it had been there all along but Jason was only noticing it right at that second. He even had the taste of it inside his mouth.

The wooden carriage wheels went *snicker* and *snap* as they bucked in and out of the ruts in the road.

Jason glanced up, hoping against hope that Lady Gweniveere wouldn't be looking at him.

She wasn't.

Her stare remained unmoved from the cool glass of the windowpane.

Should Jason run?

Hadn't Lady Gweniveere—all by herself, without so much as the need for assistance from a moustache-twiddling man—outed herself as a murderer?

. . . Or were Jason's powers of interpretation somewhat off the mark?

Jason noticed the mistletoe which hung up above the doors to the carriage.

Yes, it *was* Christmas. Of course it was . . . though sometimes he found it easy to forget.

For some reason—and maybe it was down to all those Dickensian images of Festivity which he had absorbed through the early stages of his life—Jason couldn't quite reconcile Christmas completely unless there was snow falling outside, tinsel strung up all over, and blinking, multi-coloured lights wherever there was a notable gap to fill.

But Christmas was beside the point.

For the time being.

Murder was afoot . . . or, at least, had most certainly *been* afoot in this particular 'Spiritual Past'.

The carriage came to a stop.

Without a word between them, Jason and Lady Gweniveere disembarked.

Lady Gweniveere held back a couple of moments, allowing Jason to slip past her, and so that he would have the opportunity to stand outside the carriage and offer her a helping hand down.

When Jason stepped off the carriage, he felt the give of gravel beneath the soles of his rugged hiking boots. They were in a driveway. He helped Lady Gweniveere down from the carriage.

As he absorbed the enormous, white-painted mansion which had emerged silently from the rolling, midnight foothills, he wondered if taking his eyes off a murderer (murderess?) was a particularly good idea.

Lights were lit in the mansion, and Jason could make out a tinselled wreath with candles flickering away at regular intervals. The air smelled of holly and pine, and also roasting pork, the last of which—despite Jason's vegetarian tendencies—smelled *Very Good Indeed.*

Although, as Jason had already established from before with Dougleglass, all this Channelling work really had a habit of making a fellow hungry.

Jason turned back to Lady Gweniveere who, he saw, was trying—and actually *failing*—to conceal a wide-eyed smile.

Without looking at Jason, she addressed him, saying, "Now we can fulfil *my* dreams."

Jason wasn't really sure what to make of this . . . or *any* of this for that matter.

In the entrance hall, Jason immediately felt himself being swept to one side by Lady Gweniveere.

Before Jason could so much as get himself an eyeful of his surroundings—let alone enjoy a couple of notes which emanated from an unseen string quartet—Lady Gweniveere had ushered him off into a side room which was located through a door from the hall.

Suddenly, Jason found himself surrounded by coats and attendants: bow-tied and expressionless; ploughing about like determined ants.

Especially determined ants.

Lady Gweniveere did not pause as she whisked Jason along,
keeping him from gawping at the mink, fox—*ermine?*—fur as he
passed by.

Sure, Jason knew not a lot about coats, admittedly, but he
could admire decent craftsmanship in the same way he admired
a finely compiled few lines of code in a language he couldn't
quite yet comprehend.

Lady Gweniveere finally delivered Jason to what turned out
to be a tiny little drawing room.

She met Jason's eye for a heart-stopping moment—one of
those moments which can only really be brought on from the
knowledge of exchanging glances with a maniac . . . or—at the
very least—a *murderer*. She held up a now-ungloved finger.

It was bone-white.

"Just a moment, please," she said, and slipped out of the
small drawing room, leaving Jason all on his lonesome.

A large window looked down on the gradual slope of the
gravel driveway they'd climbed to get here. Jason saw that the
driveway was lined, on either side, by conifer trees—they *were*
conifer trees, weren't they?—and that, since they'd decamped
from the carriage, the moon had gone and disappeared behind a
whole bunch of frumpy clouds.

Now that Jason thought about it, he was certain that he
could see very fine—*delicate*—snowflakes fluttering down from
the night sky.

He turned back into the drawing room, took in the walnut

bookshelves, stuffed to bursting with leather volumes; sprinkled with dust. There was a fire blazing away; its flames crackling as it consumed the hefty logs stacked on the grate within.

Jason speculated that he would've been *perfectly* happy to live exclusively in that room. He wouldn't have needed so much as a bed or a desk.

The kind-hearted, home-comfort of the room appealed to him.

Lady Gweniveere returned momentarily.

In her left hand, she carried a slick, black suede bag which was the shape of a suit.

Sure enough—Jason couldn't say that he was disappointed— Lady Gweniveere opened the bag and showed the tuxedo to Jason.

Although Jason was certain that he should've been thinking of any of a million things right then; all he could quite summon from himself was a vague hope that it would fit him okay.

For some reason—entirely alien to Jason—he found himself really looking forward to the night ahead.

Even if he was condemned to share it with a murderer.

AN OVERWHELMING OCCASION

J*ason's feet hardly touched the ground* from the second that
Lady Gweniveere helped the jacket onto his shoulders to
the moment he found himself—all of a sudden—standing
among a whole group of well-perfumed, and immaculately
pruned, gentlemen and ladies.

Jason absorbed first the enormous room, with white plaster
and cornices coming out of its ears . . . if halls had *had* ears,
that was . . .

The glass ceiling towered far above. Jason made out the
snowflakes smudging themselves up against it. When he brought
his focus downward—he kind of had to considering the speed
his feet were moving—he absorbed the slickly polished, black-
and-white tiles.

Although Jason didn't test his theory—he moved *far* too
quickly to test anything—he imagined he could have seen his
own reflection in the black tiles.

The faces—to Jason—really weren't much more than blurs. But he somehow developed a sort of Frankenstein's monster conglomeration of their features: the shining male cheeks, sun-kissed by work in the colonies, or else reddened by the wind from hunting; or whatever else it was that the deeply mysterious upper-crust got up to. The women all had powdered complexions, their eye shadow ranging a whole spectrum of colours and tones, made up so as to coordinate with their dresses.

The perfumes were a stickier issue.

Literally.

It felt almost as if Jason was breathing in some sort of thick ooze, all smothered in lavender and peaches and—*was it?* —sandalwood.

Jason really wanted to cough long and hard, but, in the present company, it was clearly not an option.

Jason did his best, feeling the cold fingernails of Lady Gweniveere clinging tight to his forearm. It was almost as if the suit which he wore offered no protection whatsoever.

He could feel his skin being squeezed beneath her fingernails.

Questions seemed to bombard Jason from just about every conceivable angle and direction.

Nearby, Jason imagined the sawing of a string quartet to be a group of Satan Spawn all tuning up for some kind of demented performance.

Before Jason could become totally overwhelmed, however, he felt Lady Gweniveere give him a squeeze on the arm which he instinctively read as meaning he should move them away.

And so Jason did.

Lady Gweniveere guided Jason about the crowded hall, past

the jolly, bald old men with their round, portly stomachs exploding over the tops of their cummerbunds.

Jason made a mental note to avoid *that* particular wardrobe choice when—*if*—he achieved that age back in the Real World.

Just as Jason believed that he had finally escaped this crowded hall, he found Lady Gweniveere sweeping them down onto *another* group of people all chortling away to themselves.

And much the same sensory overload transpired for a second time.

When the latest demonic meet-and-greet was over with, Jason found himself being 'led' away from the large hall.

Out—*finally*—into a much more sedate corridor which ran alongside.

The corridor—like the hall they had just left behind—was wall-to-wall white plaster. There was a good helping of cornices here too. The most distinctive feature of the corridor, though, was the emerald-green, thick carpet which swept on along beneath Jason's feet.

Jason attempted to keep his focus forward, but it was much trickier than he might've imagined. Lady Gweniveere really was tugging him along at a fair old whack.

Somehow, Jason managed to draw together enough puff in his lungs to get some words out through his lips. "Where . . ." he began. "Where're we *going?*"

Lady Gweniveere dragged him along behind her, and then up a narrow staircase, lined with more than a dozen oil paintings of the—*apparently former*—owners of the mansion.

Although there was no doubt Lady Gweniveere had a decent number of years on Jason, she didn't appear to be having the same issues with exasperation which Jason was currently suffering . . . he *knew* that he should've gone and joined a gym when he could've got the early-bird discount.

As they ploughed on up the staircase, Lady Gweniveere muttered, over her shoulder, "We're going to say goodbye to the man I love."

Jason could sincerely find nothing to say.

Up on the next floor, the air suddenly got a touch breezy.

When Jason looked down, he noticed the thick, emerald-green carpets had given way to stone.

He got to wondering if—*perhaps*—the whole mansion featured stone beneath the carpets . . . could this be a castle?

What even was the definition of a castle?

Jason really had no clue.

Lady Gweniveere led Jason along the stone floor until they emerged in an exterior passageway.

When Jason caught Lady Gweniveere's face in profile, he saw that there was nothing so much as *approaching* a smile on her face. She looked sour—down-trodden even.

Jason had a sort of half thought of wanting to be able to say something to cheer her up.

But, in the end, he said nothing.

Because a voice sounded up ahead.

"Stop or I'll shoot!"

For the first time in their acquaintance, Lady Gweniveere's grip became overbearing.

He felt her dig her fingernails right down deep into his skin, almost as if the only way in which Lady Gweniveere could feel tranquil again was by using Jason's bones as a stress-relief ball.

Jason stared out into the darkness, following Lady Gweniveere's gaze until he realised that Lady Gweniveere's gaze was skittering all over the place too.

She had about as much of an idea where the voice had come from as Jason did.

"Who goes there?" came the voice of the potential gunman, out of the black.

Lady Gweniveere's lip quivered slightly, and Jason felt her tremble a little against his skin.

It was then he realised, here and now, that it was his responsibility to step in—as a Channeller—and see if he couldn't help things on their way.

"Uh, just a pair from the party," Jason said.

Even to his own ears, Jason could sense the wobble in his voice. He truly wished he could—*somehow*—exorcise that unsteadiness from his voice once and for all.

The potential gunman was apparently thinking things over in his dark spot . . . wherever that was exactly. Then—rather quickly—he made up his mind. "You sound common."

Jason found himself looking back at Lady Gweniveere as if they'd prearranged to gaze at one another.

"You service staff, or wha'?" the gunman went on.

Jason glanced to Lady Gweniveere, searching for some kind of a clue . . . unfortunately for Jason, though, there wasn't one forthcoming.

So he decided to improvise.

"Yes," Jason said, "service staff—escorting the good lady here to . . ."

And then Jason was on the receiving end of a sharp elbow in the ribcage from Lady Gweniveere.

At first he thought it was because he'd said something wrong, but—in the end—it was a ploy to get him to double over so that she could whisper in his ear.

"You're here to see the prisoner," she said.

Jason remained doubled over a couple of seconds longer and then he straightened—perhaps, in retrospect considering the gunman—a touch too abruptly.

Still, at least no shot rang through the night.

"What was that?" the gunman asked. "Didn't quite catch the end of what you was saying."

Jason remembered himself, this time not requiring the previous nudge-slash-elbow in the ribs.

"We're here to see the prisoner," Jason said, confidently, firmly.

Without missing a beat, the gunman replied, "Well, you can't —on orders of the Lord."

As Jason turned back into Lady Gweniveere, looking for their next move, she grabbed a fistful of Jason's shirt, yanked him close to her and said—in a hoarse voice—"*Run!*"

DANGER

A *gunshot rang out.*
It deafened Jason temporarily.

And then the ringing started up.

It echoed endlessly about his skull.

Jason's Darwinian reflexes had never been up to all that much—not even at the best of times—and he certainly would've bought it if it hadn't been for Lady Gweniveere shoving him hard in the belly.

Knocking him flat to the ground.

Jason felt the hard, flat surface of the stone beneath him. The chill of it tingled his skin. He could feel his heart pounding in his ribcage, and his eyeballs felt almost as if they could roll right out of their sockets.

Jason had not Idea One what was going on here.

Right as Jason thought he might have to make some sort of a noticeable decision-slash-action, Lady Gweniveere clenched her hold on his shirt a touch firmer and eased him toward her. "Come on," she said in a strained whisper.

Another shot rang out in the night sky.

Another.

Jason's heart jolted with each renewed burst from the gun, and each time he assured himself, afresh, that this time—*this time*—he certainly would be biting it.

But, somehow, he didn't.

He clung to life.

Jason had always been stubborn like that.

With Lady Gweniveere's guidance, he sort of 'wormed' his way across the stone floor and—hopefully—out of danger . . . at least Lady Gweniveere seemed to be fairly confident of just where she was leading him.

After about ten minutes of scuffling, Lady Gweniveere brought their crawling escape to a halt.

When Jason turned his gaze to her, he saw that she held her finger to her lips, gesturing for him to be silent. She indicated that Jason should stand.

And Jason—the gullible berk he was—did just as she instructed.

But, thankfully, and unlike pretty much every minor character in pretty much every action film ever made, Jason didn't find himself with a bullet in his limbs, chest and/or brain.

Apparently seeing that she had guided them to safety, Lady Gweniveere also stood up.

She glanced at Jason with brilliantly bright eyes, accompanied by a gleaming smile. It was almost as if, in the space of a few minutes, she had become several years younger . . . considering how much Jason really knew about all that was going on, she might well have done.

"We've got to be quick," she said, grabbing hold of Jason's hands, intertwining her fingers with his own. "There's no time," she said. "The guard will be back soon—with company."

When Jason heard this, he couldn't resist glancing back over his shoulder, though, of course, there was nothing much to see.

They proceeded along, through an archway, down another stone corridor, until they came upon a thick, wooden door.

This—Jason could infer—was where the aforementioned 'prisoner' was being held.

For a moment, Jason wondered just why Lady Gweniveere wouldn't shove her way on in through the door, after all, they had been through some—not inconsiderable—peril to arrive here.

And then Jason saw why.

On the sturdy wooden door, there was a hefty—though quite rusted—padlock dangling down. As if Jason was a locksmith—rather than an aspiring programmer—Lady Gweniveere looked to him.

She wasn't best pleased that he could only give a vague shrug in response.

"What now?" Jason said.

Lady Gweniveere glanced about.

At first, Jason thought she was attempting to locate the key.

Instead, though, it turned out that she was merely checking to see if the coast was clear.

As far as Jason could tell, it was.

Lady Gweniveere snuck up close to the wooden door, and, in a firm voice, said, "Darling?"

From within, there was a series of shuffling sounds.

"Darling? It's me."

More shuffling.

Jason—never having been anything like the adventurous sort —could already feel as if some invisible hand was jabbing his back with searing-hot needles.

He was almost certain that somebody was standing by, ready to tell him off for doing something naughty.

Disobeying authority had never been one of Jason's strong suits.

He actually had a physical reaction to disobedience.

Jason turned his attention back to the door—and to Lady Gweniveere.

From the other side of the door, Jason heard a husky, clearly brow-beaten, voice.

". . . Gwenny?"

In that moment, despite everything, Jason felt a tickling sensation inside his ribcage.

Almost like he wanted to burst out laughing.

That was another thing about disobeying authority, he often broke out into hysterical giggles.

As far as endearing, star-crossed-lover nicknames went, 'Gwenny' was really quite an amusing one.

A few seconds passed.

Jason couldn't keep himself from letting out a giggle. He felt the full force of Lady Gweniveere's concerned stare and—Jason was certain—the man on the other side of the door was just as confused about what was going on.

Who was this giddy sod accompanying his lover?

After another few seconds, Jason's interruption was apparently forgotten. The voice on the other side of the door sounded once again and Lady Gweniveere returned her attention to it.

"Gwenny? Please," the voice went on. "You've got to go—you *must* go—if they find you here they shall . . . they shall . . ."

Lady Gweniveere pressed her wrinkled fingers up against the padlocked wooden door, and Jason wondered if her lover on the other side might not be doing the same. Although Jason knew next to *nothing* about happiness—let alone *love*—he could tell that these two upper-class characters had been greatly happy together.

No, surely *were* happy together.

So who was he to complain?

"Don't worry," Lady Gweniveere said in reply, "if it's the last thing that I ever do, I shall touch you again—I will reach out and stroke your cheeks, stare into your chocolate eyes."

A long pause as the person on the other side of the door absorbed the intricacies of this statement. Then, "There's no way in . . . or out."

THE LOCKED ROOM

I t *was then* that Jason heard the commotion over his shoulder, the stamping procession of clearly dozens of booted feet. Although Jason knew it really couldn't be so, he imagined that he could smell the odour of gunpowder from the rifles the guardsmen surely carried.

It brought a bitter taste onto the tip of his tongue.

A shudder passed through the stone slabs beneath his feet.

He waited for the shouting voices, or maybe he was just waiting for the sound of gunfire.

Whatever he waited for, he assured himself that it would occur soon.

Jason looked to Lady Gweniveere who, understandably, was somewhat startled by this latest development. Although, in truth, Jason really couldn't see how it had come across as unexpected.

Had she really believed that, after firing off a pair of shots into the darkness after a pair of intruders, the gunman would just draw a line under the entire incident?

If only . . .

Jason, realising that, once again, he was supposed to be some kind of beacon of light, decided that it was up to him to take action.

And so he did.

Jason lined up a shoulder barge on the wooden, padlocked door. Even as he set himself through the motions, he really couldn't believe exactly what he was doing . . . which was probably just as well seeing as he had always seen himself as the poster child for Cowardly Weakling.

This time, though, he only went and surprised himself.

As Jason felt his shoulder make contact with the wooden door, the wood splintered beneath the force. He felt the jagged shards pass into his skin.

And that was only the start of the pain, as he would discover later on.

He busted through the door only to be surprised that it was at least as dark inside as it had been out. And perhaps that was part of the reason for his surprise as he barrelled right into someone.

Jason knocked the 'someone' flat on his back.

And then lay on top of him, pinning him to the stone floor.

For several of Jason's many rapid heartbeats, they lay there, neither of them apparently all that keen to converse.

Soon, though, there was little option to do anything else.

The stamp of marching boots veritably invaded the sound-scape of the tight, wall-to-floor stone room. Before Jason could think up anything really significant to say, he felt Lady

Gweniveere launch herself into his side, barging him clear of her beau.

Jason was content just to sort of roll off to the side.

He couldn't help but overhear the muttered conversation between Lady Gweniveere and her lover.

It *was* a small room, after all . . .

"Dearest," Lady Gweniveere said, "you wouldn't believe what I've had to get through so we could meet—just one more time."

Her words were hurried and, clearly, reflecting the sense of peril which clung to the room like a particularly bad odour.

"You never should've risked it," her lover replied.

Jason could just about make out the basic features of the couple now that his eyes had somewhat adjusted to the gloom, and now that his adrenalin had let off just a touch . . . just enough to allow him to feel the biting pain in his shoulder, in any case.

The man—Lady Gweniveere's beau—looked haggard, and his clothes hung off him as if they were a couple of sizes too large. Loose skin hung down from his throat.

Jason couldn't shake the impression that, perhaps, Lady Gweniveere's beau had once been rather portly. This incarnation was thinned down somewhat, and not necessarily for the worse.

A shame, really, that he was condemned to death.

"We must jump, dear," Lady Gweniveere said, helping her beau to his feet.

Her beau wobbled a good few times before truly finding his balance.

His shoulders stuck out a little jagged from the tattered sleeves of his jacket-slash-rags, but other than this minor affliction, Jason didn't feel it necessary to revise his opinion of Lady Gweniveere's beau's appearance.

Jason missed Lady Gweniveere's statement at first pass.

But then it sunk in.

We must jump . . .

He realised the two of them had moved past the stage of merely *coming to terms* with Lady Gweniveere's call to action.

Now the two of them were gazing across the cell at a turret-shaped window which—even to Jason's slender-framed perspective—looked like it would be something of a tight squeeze.

And he could tell, just by looking, that the other two would have a much harder time getting through the gap.

But was that even the real issue here?

. . . There *was* the small matter of the 'jumping-out-the-window' part.

Was that really what needed to be done?

Wasn't it within Jason's job description, as Channeller, to be a sort of voice of reason—the one to fix all issues which might influence the Unquiet currently resigned to his responsibility?

Lady Gweniveere and her beau were already making for the window which would—*surely*—be far too much of a squeeze to accommodate the auto-defenestration of any one of them.

But, it seemed, with the tramping boots becoming louder than peals of thunder, there simply wouldn't be another option.

Lady Gweniveere and her beau had graduated from 'just looking' to 'actively attempting' to get out of the window.

There really wasn't much more Jason could do . . . save seeing how he could pitch in.

And so pitch in he did.

At first Jason was sort of at a loose end as to how he

might help these star-crossed lovers get on out through the window. Through whichever tool of logic had been employed, it was the beau who was trying to get out the window first.

And they were both clearly struggling to get him up and at it . . . so to speak.

The main issue, so far as Jason could see, was that Lady Gweniveere's beau was—how should he put it?—on the *shorter* side of things.

And, therefore, the part of getting out the window which he was most struggling with was the leap up to the sill.

This—Jason decided, putting his Channeller's cap on—was where he could pitch in.

So, feeling in a somewhat helpful mood, Jason shifted on up beside the pair.

The sound of tramping boots was the loudest it'd been yet.

The barking voices reached a pitch which suggested—if possessor of said voice carried a firearm—somebody was bound to get shot.

Jason cupped his hands, forming a makeshift—but extremely serviceable—*boost*.

Lady Gweniveere's beau stepped up onto Jason's clasped hands, reached out for the window and set about escaping.

He slipped out of the window much more easily than Jason would've expected.

Swoosh!

No exaggeration . . .

Off into the night.

. . . *Down* into the night.

With a tremor passing through the stone floor now and an

odd, musky scent filling Jason's nostrils, he committed the same action to aid Lady Gweniveere out through the window.

Just like her beau—*swoosh!*—and out she went.

The marching boots and the scent of gunpowder suddenly transformed into dozens of beardy—and extremely grumpy-looking—faces.

All of them with their guns—*rifles?*—pointed at Jason's chest.

Realising that there was little choice, Jason acted.

He hurled himself at the 'window'.

And—*swoosh!*—out he went too.

JUMPING OUT A WINDOW

B eing *a man* infinitely better-suited to the indoors, Jason had never had much time for theoretical imaginings. Theoretical imaginings like, 'What might it feel like to plunge an enormous drop?'

Much less, 'How might it feel like to plunge an enormous drop *after* having broken into—then out of—a jail cell, while evading nasty men with guns?'

Jason supposed, if he had had such time for frivolities, he might've experienced such a situation—or one very much like it —in a video game.

But he hadn't . . . so there it was.

To say that Jason was terrified as he took the plunge down from the window, as he felt the chill of wind sting his cheeks, strip away any taste that might've been on his tongue; forcibly remove any smells that might've lingered a little longer than was polite in his nostrils; flood his ears with an endless, rippling gale .

. . would really not be doing justice to the mind-melting that was going on within the inner recesses of his skull.

His brain was—very quickly—turning to sludge.

And the gloom below which, even in Jason's rapidly snatched fantasies, only ever contained, in the very best scenarios: lush, long grass.

Although Jason hardly lived all that much in the Real World, his mind did prompt him that—*really*—grass wasn't going to do all that much for him.

Or his continuing mortality.

Strangely, though, as Jason felt himself plunge what might've easily been a hundred or so metres, he felt his falling body arrest its acceleration.

He was slowing.

Gradually.

But he *was* slowing

Jason almost had the urge to do a fist-pump—just a *tiny* one —but he managed to talk himself out of it. He knew all about counting chickens before they'd hatched.

Many a piece of software which had once appeared so promising had—metaphorically—laughed in his face when testing time rolled around.

But Jason *was* slowing.

And soon—despite this internal cockiness, and expecting an equal dose of karma in recompense—Jason was floating in mid-air.

It might've been a pleasant feeling if it hadn't been for the cocking of rifle hammers . . . or whatever it was that went *click-click* on rifles.

Jason really had next-to-no interest in guns of any sort.

And, even then, there might've been some prospect of relaxation if not for the rattle of bullets suddenly all around—like demented, pointed hailstones.

But as those bullets did rattle about him, Jason had something of a realisation.

None of the bullets had—so far—actually struck him.

Was it a matter of luck?

. . . Or was it something else?

Jason saw no reason for coming down one way or the other.

He was—after all—still in some kind of peril.

As Jason stood about there in mid-air, an even more surreal sensation than it sounded, he couldn't help but notice his feet gently, as if guided by angelic hands, drifting downward, approaching the long grasses below.

And—*oh!*—could he ever see those long grasses now, as the stray bullets shot them all up in clods of mud. He could smell the wet dirt on the air, and he caught that lush, *grassy* taste at the back of his mouth.

It might've been quite a pleasant pair of sensations if not for the maniacs with firearms above him.

Soon enough, though, and without so much as a single bullet flinging itself through his spine—severing every last one of his nerves as it went—Jason felt his feet land firmly in that *mythical* 'shoulder-width apart' distance his PE teachers would always bleat on about.

Jason had never been all that great at PE . . .

He stared off into the darkness, as ever, in search of a clue as to what Fate expected him to do next.

But Fate, like always, it seemed, wasn't receptive to Jason's desires.

So Jason did what he always did when he had no idea what to do.

In life, as in programming, he wandered off in one direction or another.

And just as such exploration often seemed to bear fruit in computer-based worlds of Jason's creation, it did so now.

But it could quite easily have been all so different if Jason hadn't heard Lady Gweniveere call out to him, clearly somewhat alarmed.

On another, less fortunate evening, Jason would quite easily have tripped right over the couple, lying tangled upon the flattened long grasses at his feet.

But he didn't break his neck.

And, for that, Jason was glad.

Life, as he'd learned long ago, was all about the little victories.

Jason crouched down to the Unquiet currently under his *de facto* supervision.

He looked the two of them over.

Lady Gweniveere held her beau in her arms.

Jason only realised about a second later that Lady Gweniveere's beau was wounded.

A large, dark spot marked his tunic where a bullet had penetrated him.

When Jason turned his attention to Lady Gweniveere, he saw that her legs had crumpled beneath her. The fall from the window, high above, had broken her bones.

Jason couldn't help thinking that he'd gone and messed this whole thing up something rotten.

Not much he could do about it now, though, save go crawling

to the old lady in the duffel coat and ask her to allow him a fresh run at this Spiritual Past.

Strangely, with the odd *pop* from a rifle up above, Jason saw that both Lady Gweniveere and her beau were smiling.

From ear-to-ear.

One of those kinds of shared smiles which would often put Jason on edge, if only because he was so accustomed to those smiles representing some kind of private joke at his expense.

This time, though, he didn't mind at all.

Maybe it was because he was certain that they *weren't* laughing at his expense.

Or, maybe, it was because Jason just didn't care anymore who laughed at him.

With nothing else pressing to do here, Jason crouched down beside his pet Unquiet and fixed Lady Gweniveere with an apologetic gaze.

What *else* could he do?

"I'm sorry," Jason said, and then, not really all that gifted when it came to reading social situations, he added, "It wasn't my idea to jump out the window."

Even through their obvious pain, their pallid complexions, Lady Gweniveere and her beau chuckled back at him.

Maybe the joke was on Jason after all.

"Oh, dear," Lady Gweniveere said, a pair of tears escaping her eyes and lolling down her cracked, wrinkled skin. "You really *are* new at all of this, aren't you?"

Jason thought it best to keep quiet.

"We're together," Lady Gweniveere went on, "at last, we are together."

Jason looked from Lady Gweniveere's smiling face to her beau's.

Lady Gweniveere continued, "I was on my way to see him for the last time when the highwayman arrived." She glanced back to her beau who seemed struck by a sort of grimacing smile and who was clearly in such a great deal of pain that he could no longer form words . . . at least not words which would've made any sense.

In a way, Jason supposed it was a bit like those days when he spent every waking moment flying through line-upon-line of code. His mind would become so stuffed full of whatever programming language he happened to be utilising that particular day that normal, everyday human speech would become a simply impossible task.

That was how it was for Lady Gweniveere's beau right now.

Jason could see it in his eyes.

He looked back to Lady Gweniveere. She stroked her beau's hair as if he was a favourite cat.

Lady Gweniveere continued, "He took the blame for me—accident, but, still, murder . . ."

The way Lady Gweniveere trailed off wasn't particularly reassuring.

But he could make out the distant *thump* of boots.

Guards approaching.

There wasn't much time, but, somehow, Jason realised it really didn't matter all that much any longer.

Lady Gweniveere went on, "It was a summer's day, and much like any other. The sun was setting on the grounds of the mansion house which my husband had inherited as part of my dowry. A tangerine glow just dwindling on the horizon. And I . . .

well . . . he *and* I"—she glanced downward to indicate her beau, dying ever so quietly in her lap—"we had just had an argument, one of the only times we had truly had any sort of falling-out. My husband, he had been sitting in the conservatory of the home, in his favourite wicker chair, staring out through the glass, into the garden. An empty tumbler of whisky sitting beside him, just waiting for me to freshen it up."

Here Lady Gweniveere's breath hitched in her throat and she paused for several moments, apparently waiting for it to return to her. "We bought the hemlock a week before."

She met Jason's gaze dead on in a way which seemed to say— at least to Jason's socially retarded reception—*'don't judge me'* . . . though, if Jason couldn't judge a self-confessed murderer, then he wondered who he rightly *could* judge.

"My husband had been awfully unwell for such a long time, and—really—his illness was a blessing, a ray of hope coming through the grisly, grey fog of our loveless marriage.

"But he clung on. He kept *on* clinging on."

Lady Gweniveere's eyes drifted away from Jason's once more, and Jason noted the slight rise in volume as the guards were—no doubt—being instructed to search the grounds for the intruders.

To ensure that they were truly dead and gone.

Lady Gweniveere shook her head. "You have no idea what it is to live a life of dead-eyed smiles, to wake up in a distant and boxy bedroom alone, and to dress yourself every day only to have to face another loveless moment in a string of loveless moments which—*linked together*—must somehow qualify for one's life."

Although Jason couldn't say that he could personally identify with this particular sentiment—he could certainly give some kind of empathy a good, solid try.

Lady Gweniveere continued, "And since my husband was sick he began to forget himself—he was nothing more than a shell of a man. Why"—here Lady Gweniveere glanced to her beau—"we would quite easily be in and around the house. Once . . . once . . ."

Jason recognised a slight drop in what had been a previously rigid—if not *uncrackable*—exterior.

Maybe it was the knowledge that death crept close by which allowed Lady Gweniveere to drop her guard at long last.

"Once my husband even happened upon my bedroom while we lay clutched in one another's arms beneath the sheets. He did not notice—blathered something incomprehensible—and then took his leave, never mentioning anything about it. But we wanted more, we knew that it was not the done thing for us to tread about in the shadows; awaiting death—*his* death.

"And so, that afternoon, in his freshened glass of whisky, I administered the poison and stood by with my heart fluttering in my chest as he drank . . . but it was not at all how I had imagined, he did not go quietly—not an inch of it.

"Perhaps I mixed up the dosage, or maybe I left the poison under some unsuitable circumstance. Whatever the reason, I could only play the observer as my husband writhed about the floor of the conservatory; unable to contain himself, and yet still clinging to his life with both hands."

Lady Gweniveere trembled slightly and—even in the moonlight—Jason could tell that her complexion had turned even paler.

And why wouldn't it have done?

What she described to Jason was positively horrific.

Lady Gweniveere went on, "I did not know what to do and

so I retired to my bedroom—not to sleep, for even in the large, country house, I could hear his blathering, the odd breakage of porcelain or some other ornamental trifle.

"I was thankful that I had had enough foresight as to plan the assassination on a weekend when the household staff were absent—there was only Mrs Myers, the housekeeper, in her cottage halfway across the grounds, and, being deaf as a post, unlikely to overhear anything short of an earthquake."

Jason noticed Lady Gweniveere's beau gulp for breath.

Out in the never-ending darkness which surrounded them—punctuated only by the odd window; illuminated by sallow candlelight—he heard a twig snap, the mumbling of voices.

The guards closing in on them.

Soon there would be no escape.

Not for Jason's star-crossed lovers.

Apparently noting her surroundings, despite her rapidly worsening injuries, Lady Gweniveere quickened to the conclusion of the story.

"I lay in bed until I observed the morning light creeping up the horizon, and I did not move a muscle until I heard the cockerel's cry. But—when I did move—I moved quickly, without a second thought.

"No hesitation.

"When I descended to the conservatory, I saw that my husband lay sprawled out on his front and—by God—I would've thought him dead if it hadn't been for the twitch of one of his fingers; his palm overturned and facing up to the glass ceiling.

"Up to the heavens."

The voices about them grew louder still.

They had maybe a minute, if they were lucky.

They *would* be found out, wouldn't they?

Lady Gweniveere snatched what could—quite easily—have been her final breath.

Then she concluded her tale.

"I snatched up a nearby lamp—I bludgeoned him until he no longer moved."

The way she spoke now, her voice was so cool, so detached.

"Then—together—we buried him in the garden; there seemed no other option. We told all acquaintances—all family and friends—that he had passed away at home; and that such a quiet ceremony was in keeping with my husband's will. It wasn't difficult to have a false death certificate drawn up. Nobody complained. Although the secret had been duly kept, it was really a widely known fact that my husband was no longer the man he had once been. That he had grown *weak* in old age—his death was not . . . *unanticipated.*"

Lady Gweniveere blinked a pair of times in such a way that suggested she might've been able—once upon a time—to summon tears on demand.

But now there was nothing at all.

"For a while, we lived quite happily and, although questions were occasionally asked, they were never put in a *vulgar* fashion."

Jason glanced about them, feeling his heart beating harder still.

Then he turned back to Lady Gweniveere.

"But then it all changed," she continued. "Fifteen years passed, we were accustomed to our new life—we dared believe that our twilight years would be our own . . . and then, a new gardener was digging in the wrong place, and it all tumbled down."

She paused for a second.

"For good."

Jason could hear the voices of the guards mere paces away now.

But none of this shook Lady Gweniveere from finishing her story.

Lady Gweniveere clutched her beau's hand to her chest.

Jason knew that her beau's life was quickly departing.

Jason didn't wish to utter so much as a word. He could make out the clutched sobs beneath Lady Gweniveere's breath. This was the most private of moments and here he was invading it.

Jason turned away from the two of them, sort of assuming that they would forget he was even there . . . but, no . . . Lady Gweniveere had one final thing to tell Jason.

And Jason was all ears.

"He took the blame," Lady Gweniveere said, "all of the responsibility for the murder—and I *so* wanted to see him the last time before his execution; only fate got in the way." She paused for a moment and if she did sob it was well and truly out of Jason's earshot. "And now I have—*now* have made things right. *Thank you*," she added, her words almost a whisper.

At first, Jason believed that she was thanking her dearly— and *very recently departed*—beau.

But when Jason turned to look at her, he saw she was staring at him.

Her eyes wet with tears.

From somewhere in the distance, there was a gunshot.

And then blackness.

Nothing.

A JOB WELL DONE?

J ason's feet seemed to be weightless for a long, long while.

He believed he would continue to float about, unable to ever find his way back to his own world—to his own time—ever again.

But, then, slowly, it all returned.

The tiny *buzz* of static from the PA system within the bus-station waiting room. The wall-to-wall concrete. That *stench* of disinfectant, accompanied, of course, by that dry sensation; that medicinal taste at the back of his mouth.

And a slight chill.

No, scratch *that*.

An *almighty* chill.

Jason's teeth chattered together so hard he worried the enamel might split.

It took him another few seconds to get his body back under full control, and, when he did, he absorbed the waiting room.

The man in the chicken suit was still there.

The cute girl his age was still there.

And the elderly lady in the duffel coat was *still there*.

Jason switched his attention back to the wooden, painfully uncomfortable benches.

His eyeballs, having become accustomed to the rather dim, oil lanterns—and then the *night*—seemed to almost catch fire in the brightness of the high-powered, fluorescent strip bulbs.

Squinting so that he wouldn't cry all down his cheeks, he switched a quick glance over to the place on the wooden bench where he'd been sitting previously.

His bag—with his travelling laptop presumably still inside— was where it had been before. He'd left it behind this time, unlike his first trip with Dougleglass.

Truth be told, there didn't seem to be much use for computers in the Spiritual Past; although it pained Jason to admit it.

If his travelling laptop *had* gone missing from the bus-station waiting room then it would've been a very narrow list of suspects to choose from . . . if push came to shove, he personally would've chosen to accuse the man in the mangy-looking chicken suit.

But, then again, Jason had always had a fairly low tolerance for Weirds—and the man in the chicken suit certainly qualified as one of *those*.

Not receiving any order or direction from the old lady specifying he should do the opposite, Jason padded over to his fairly tranquil spot in the waiting room.

. . . At least he had *hoped* it would turn out to be a 'tranquil' spot.

It hadn't turned out that way in the end.

All this Spiritual Past business really did rub him up the wrong way.

Pity that he had—apparently—no say in his involvement with it.

Jason had hardly sat back down on the wooden bench when another shudder, brought on by the chilly draught blowing about the waiting room, caused him to nearly lose control of his body once more. The only way he could force himself to stop shuddering was by clamping his jaw shut tight.

And, even then, he required the assistance of both hands to keep his teeth from breaking out in that same spasm all over again.

Jason knew that—in his bag—he had a warm fleece buried somewhere near the bottom.

Despite the mild winter, what he'd seen of it, some sort of horse sense had kicked in as he'd been heading on out through the door to his university room.

Some deep—perhaps *long-buried*—knowledge that:

CHRISTMAS = COLD

If only Jason could somehow loosen his hands from their current predicament—clamping his jaw shut.

Jason felt as if someone was watching him.

He glanced around.

The old lady in the duffel coat was staring at him.

Again.

The screen showing the bus departures was just as switched off as it had been previously.

It didn't seem that Jason would be getting out of this thing before Fate—or whatever the hell someone might call it—was done with him.

Just like she had before, the old woman in the duffel coat spoke directly into Jason's mind.

He really would've been glad to stumble on a solution that would stop her from doing so . . .

— *Congratulations, Channeller, you have assisted your second Unquiet in finding her peace.*

There was a slight pause within Jason's mind, which—in retrospect —was a very odd sensation indeed.

— *How do you feel?*

Jason studied the question in his own mind.

How *did* he feel?

On a whim, Jason had ventured on out from his perfectly serviceable university-halls room so that he might spend Christmas with his insufferable parents. And, everything else aside, he had been somewhat glad to have a little more time to think things through. Oh, sure, if Jason had gone and hopped right on a bus back home to Staplesham then he might've had the hour-or-so journey to consider the thought process which'd eventually pushed him toward going home for Christmas Eve— not to mention Christmas *itself* . . . but, then again, had Jason really had any time to think about *anything* save how to help his Unquiet find their peace?

No, actually . . .

And so, as a self-proclaimed journey of self-discovery, Jason couldn't help but feel somewhat short-changed thus far.

Sure, he got all that stuff about altruism—yeah, he'd got that crap by the time he was like eight or so, and had seen way more than his fair share of big-studio approved films based on the subject.

All that 'joy of giving' versus the 'misery of taking'.

Was this really another one of those *lessons?*

Bullshit, if it was . . .

— *No, Channeller, this has nothing to do with any of those 'lessons',*
believe me.

Jason felt a tremble pass down his spine.

His heart juddered against his ribs.

All at once he breathed in the disinfectant and tasted its dry
flavour at the back of his throat.

His hearing gave off a teeth-gnawing ringing.

The chill in the waiting room became more pronounced still,
and Jason would've killed to have his fleece simply *appear* about
his middle section. That would've sorted him right out.

But it didn't.

That was 'magic' for you; a bloody nuisance when it raised its
head, and a smug-looking, wise old cat when it didn't.

Jason had always *hated* cats.

And dogs.

Both had their relative demerits.

— *Channeller, this has nothing to offer you personally, beside deeply*
felt fulfilment and a sense of your place in the world.

While Jason scolded himself for doing so, at the same time
he couldn't stop . . . he spoke back to the old woman in the
duffel coat within his own mind, and he knew that if he had *ever*
had any sort of higher ground in this interaction—moral, or
otherwise—then he had lost it forever.

— *What do I need to fulfil me?*

There, Jason had gone and done it.

No taking it back.

Not *now.*

— *Love.*

The answer was so concise and—apparently—so unambiguous, that Jason had quite tangible and *real* trouble in saying anything in response.

What *could* he say in response?

He did think of something . . . eventually—and, much to his consternation, he spoke it out loud to himself.

Within his own mind.

— *What do I need with love?*

Even as Jason said this within his own mind, he couldn't help thinking back to his computer—the thoughts which he had attached to it.

His Computer Love.

Had this old lady, in her duffel coat, overheard all of that?

Her answer, like the previous one, was clear, unambiguous.

— *Yes.*

Jason felt a chill pass right down his spine.

He wasn't much sure he enjoyed knowing that this old woman, and—*potentially*—anyone like her, with her 'special' skillset, might be able to do the same. He really *did* need to do some research into the matter when this was all over.

If this ever ended . . .

Knowing that there was precious little he could do about where he was going next, Jason simply awaited the old woman in the duffel coat.

He awaited the next words she would speak into his mind.

— *Fear not, Channeller, because this time I shall be giving you a companion; somebody to assist you on your third, and final, assignment.*

So these were 'assignments' now?

Forgetting that the old lady in the duffel coat had spoken into his mind directly, and trying his best to forget that he had *replied* to her from within his own mind, Jason said, out loud, for anybody in the waiting room who cared to hear, "So, *who's* my companion?"

NOT ALONE

J ason couldn't help thinking to himself, *Me and my big mouth.*
And that, despite the fact, as a rule, Jason spoke to
almost no one. He went *out of his way* not to speak to
anyone . . . and yet, right here, right now, he'd gone and *asked*
for it.

Literally.

Instead of a simple, level-headed response—or, indeed—any
sort of response at all from the old woman in the duffel coat,
Jason just found himself twirling about in the midst of time and
space, or whatever it was that the blackness represented.

Maybe it was dark matter . . .

That really would be one in the eye for Mrs Michaels, his
physics teacher back at school.

The one who had told him, right to his face, that he would
never—*ever*—be a physicist . . . and, well, she hadn't been wrong.
No matter how much it pained Jason to admit it.

Ever since he had opted to take computer science, Jason had felt an odd, tightening sensation across his chest. Perhaps it was a physically manifested symptom of physics envy. Or maybe —*just maybe*—it was gas . . .

As Jason spiralled through the, increasingly chilly, *nada* he couldn't help but turn his mind to where he was going to end up next.

And, as it turned out, he really didn't have to do all that much imagining.

Because he was here.

He had *arrived.*

Snow floated down in thick, blankety sheets. It layered itself about his shoes, forming dunes all around. When Jason looked— or *attempted* to look—through the constantly falling flurries, he couldn't see a thing.

Not a *bloody* thing.

Jason did wonder why he had never got around to digging out the fleece which resided at the bottom off his backpack; why the old lady had deigned not to leave him so much as a moment, or two, so that he could fetch what would be—in this particular climate—a *very welcoming* garment.

. . . But what could Jason say about this whole experience except that it had served to reinforce—to underline and *double score*—the old assertion that, *Shit happens.*

Clutching his arms tight about his chest, and trying to instil a modicum of warmth into his poor, battered, aspiring computer programmer's body; Jason thought that he heard a sound somewhere between a thunderclap and a howl of wind.

In short, it sounded like the youthful special effects crew of some TV station with too much money, and *far* too much time, had spent a long while on finding a *really* unique sound that its particular audience would never—*ever*—forget.

That was what drifted through Jason's brain, at least, and he would stick to it.

Even under the most brutal of interrogations.

When Jason finally stopped analysing the sound and actually pivoted to see what the source had been, he was somewhat surprised.

But not overwhelmingly so.

He saw the blond girl . . . the *cute* one from the waiting room.

The old woman in the duffel coat had, after all, promised Jason not just romance, but Lurve, L-U-R-V-E, with a capital 'L'.

The blond girl's cheeks seemed almost immediately affected by the ice-cold gusts, which turned her once pearly-pink complexion an unpleasant, slightly bashful, rash-red.

But Jason still found much to admire in her.

She *was* very attractive.

Or maybe Jason was just desperate beyond comprehension or reason . . .

The blond girl had her arms crossed over her chest in one of those most defensive of postures. She also looked quite cold, and Jason speculated that she could probably do with a fleece as much as Jason. And, if he had had one, he might well have offered it to her.

Wouldn't that have been the chivalrous thing to do?

Yes, for Jason to produce—out of nowhere—a fleece and to, thereby, all at once, demonstrate that he could put others' needs before himself *and*, on top of that, suffer in silence; that really would be a fine thing to happen.

A little cold certainly wouldn't crack *these* balls of steel . . .

When Jason did his best to make soft eye contact with the girl—which, in retrospect, probably looked more like a lecherous glare—the girl merely pretended not to see him there at all.

Well, two could very well play at this game.

Jason, being an aspiring computer programmer, and the blond girl being a ghost, the two of them were well used to being looked through.

Jason settled for glancing about himself into the constantly falling snow and trying—with little-to-no success—to think *warm* thoughts.

If only . . . if *only* he'd brought his fleece . . .

As Jason did stare off into the—seemingly—thickening clouds of white which formed all around him, he began to be able to make out a shape.

Nothing *more* than a shape, mind, but it was most certainly a start.

Jason, soon enough, managed to see a sort of colour growing out of that *shape* . . . a tone which—at first—he could only really identify as being *not* white.

And then—ever so gradually—Jason managed to pick out the colouration.

Yellow.

The colour of *yellow* snow.

Perhaps it was the simple combination of yellow with white which brought on that particular comparison in Jason's mind.

But, there it was.

Yellow-snow yellow.

Not really seeing that he could manoeuvre this way or the other, Jason saw no other option but to wait for this yellowish splodge to approach.

Soon enough, the falling curtains of snow parted sufficiently for Jason to get a full idea of just what it was he was looking at.

A man in a chicken suit.

Again, thinking about it now, something of a no-brainer.

The man in the chicken suit—the blond girl aside—was the final Unquiet which would require Jason's services . . . or could it be that the old lady in the duffel coat had some trick up her sleeve?

Could it be that she had a whole stock of other Unquiet just waiting in some back room for Jason's 'expertise' in guiding them through the Spiritual Past?

What did the old woman in the duffel coat have to gain from letting Jason go?

"Trust me," the man in the chicken suit said, drawing closer, "she has to let you go sometime—it's not like you'll live forever; not like Old Mother Time."

Jason stood beleaguered for several moments.

He tried to piece together just what the chicken-suited man meant.

But then he hit upon what was—on reflection—the far larger issue in play.

"You heard my thoughts?" Jason said, perhaps not sounding as surprised as he otherwise would . . . if he hadn't had this particular party trick played on him quite so recently.

"Uh-huh," the chicken-suited man replied, equally nonchalantly.

Jason felt an out-of-place heat flush through his whole stomach. His heart skipped a couple dozen beats. And then he said, "Can . . . can *all* of you"—he stretched his mind for the nomenclature . . . if nothing else, he wanted to be sure they were singing from the same hymn sheet—"Can all of you read minds? All of you *Unquiet*, I mean."

The chicken-suited man gave a shrug. "Dunno, guess that some of us can; the ones who put their minds to it."

Quickly, Jason did a mental inventory of every thought he had had in Lady Gweniveere and Dougleglass's company.

Although there was nothing that stuck out at him, he also realised that what seemed—to him—'normal' might well be something which, if potentially spoken out loud, let alone *over-heard*, might see him locked up in some sort of mental institution.

One of those ones with the padded walls and hourly pills . . .

Finding himself stumbling onto this—somewhat depressing —mind-track, Jason caught himself.

He forced a full purge of thoughts from his mind, and yet, when he looked to the chicken-suited man, he realised he was on the receiving end of a somewhat askance glance . . . when the chicken-suited man spoke again, his voice sounded a little hesitant and Jason was sure that he was, no doubt, performing a little armchair psychoanalysis on Jason's most-recent thoughts.

Jason only noticed that the chicken-suited man had stuck his hand out for him to shake when he said, "Name's Patrick— wanna see where I died?"

"WHERE I DIED"

J ason made a very conscious effort not to think of anything at all as they trudged on through the flurries of snow with, apparently, no end in sight.

As they proceeded, Patrick chatted along in a light-hearted manner, which was to say, if Jason hadn't known Patrick was dead then he certainly wouldn't have guessed it.

The blond girl hung back from them, trudging along on their heels not having quite joined their two-man group. She had produced her headphones from somewhere and she walked along with her hands stuffed into the pockets of her coat; her head bobbing ever so slightly.

Romance didn't seem to be much on the cards, but, then again, Jason was fairly certain he was better off giving up on trying to know what was going on.

He *was* dealing with somebody called 'Old Mother Time', after all.

Patrick led Jason onward, through the blizzard, and Jason felt the ice-cold flakes rake down his cheeks. Just the sensation of the cold itself seemed enough to rob him of any sense of taste or smell. The only thing he could hear—if he could really *accurately* refer to it as a 'thing' at all—was the fearsome *brush* of the snowflakes tumbling down.

Whoever thought that snow was some kind of benign, pleasant thing really needed to have their head checked.

Shouting to be heard against the gale, Patrick said, "Thought she'd drop us somewhere in town!"

"What?!" Jason said, without thinking.

"You know!" Patrick went on. "Have us show up in town! So that we could find our way about! She went and transported us here, though! We're a good five, ten minutes out into the countryside!"

"Oh!" Jason replied, and looked about himself at the whited-out surroundings as if this statement of Patrick's lent the landscape a whole new significance.

It didn't, but it *did* afford Jason a decent perving opportunity on the blond girl . . . though he saw she was much the same as she had been before:

Headphones tightly wrapped about her ears.

Hands sunk into pockets.

Not so much as bothering to look up at Jason.

. . . And yet he could *tell* that she knew he was looking.

She was just playing coy . . . or, maybe, she just wasn't playing at all.

Everything could, quite easily, be taking place within Jason's own mind.

She was, surely, as confused about finding herself here—in this snowy domain—as Jason himself was.

Or maybe not . . .

It really *was* a never-ending stream of *what-ifs* and *what-abouts*, and Jason promised himself that he would get through with them sooner rather than later.

Jason returned his focus to his conversation with Patrick, realising that he'd allowed his end of the exchange to go slack. When Jason turned back to examine Patrick—and his chicken suit—he was grinning from ear to ear. "Think you forgot I can read minds, matey!"

"I think so, too!" Jason replied, still shouting to be heard over the gale.

And they wandered on.

As they trudged through deep snow, Jason wondered about his previous two experiences with Lady Gweniveere and Dougleglass.

It was sort of like what Patrick said, which was to say that, when Jason had ventured on out through the sliding doors of the bus station, and into the night, the world had—*somehow*—transformed before his eyes.

What'd once been the town he knew—he wouldn't quite stretch to *love*—had transformed into how it had been decades, centuries before . . . to reflect the Spiritual Past of whichever Unquiet he had happened to be 'escorting' at the time.

But this time—as Patrick had pointed out—they'd gone and

ended up in the countryside a little way out of town. And, if it wasn't awfully pleasant to have a nice, relaxing walk mingled in with perilous snowfall, it was just a little befuddling for the old brain.

Patrick brought them in through a pair of crooked streets which Jason vaguely recognised.

Although he hadn't really spent any time at all 'getting to know' this town, on his trips to-and-fro by bus, he had seen more than enough to convince him that it didn't hold any great surprises.

Patrick led them—Jason and the blond girl—along a cobble-stone street at the end of which they happened across a canal.

It was here that Jason had to admit that his quaint—perhaps a polite way of saying 'backward'—university town had beaten him to the punch in terms of surprising him.

Maybe he'd been the 'backward' one all along . . .

Now, Jason had never been the most observant fellow in the known universe—far from it—but he did find it somewhat remarkable that he had gone through his entire academic career so far and never noticed that there was a dirty, sewage-stinking canal which ran right down the middle of it.

Still, he knew that it existed now.

At least that was *something*.

Patrick stared down at the frozen surface of the canal—at the ash-grey snow which had collected on the top. He was staring at it in such a focussed way—almost a *nostalgic* way—that it immediately put Jason on edge.

Jason caught the impression that he was imminently going to be on the receiving end of a creepy story. And, sure enough, it was then that Patrick turned side-on to Jason.

"You're a very perceptive man, pal."

Right . . . Patrick could read his mind.

Oops.

"HOW I DIED ..."

Patrick got all wistful of eye—which was to say nothing of his voice, other than it couldn't possibly have fitted in any more wist without it having tried really very hard indeed.

Jason started wondering if he could maybe beat a retreat, in one direction, or the other, but then he reminded himself about the whole mind-reading thing.

This time, he didn't need any sort of a reminder from Patrick.

As Patrick loosened up his verbiage pipes, Jason snuck another, well-earned—though not a *little* snoopy—glance back at the blond girl.

Just like Jason, she seemed to be settling in for a long old haul of reminiscence.

Patrick let out a sustained breath of hot air. "This is where I died," he said, sounding a little sombre and probably not without reason. "It was a cold night, as you might well imagine."

Jason really hadn't much clue at all about what he might've imagined given the opportunity, but weather most probably wouldn't have been top of the list.

"I was dressed for a costume party." Patrick paused for several moments. "I mean to say that, back when I was alive, I didn't make a habit of dressing up like a chicken.

"A little tragic, in its own way. There're several of us Unquiet who went and died in fancy-dress costumes, only for us to spend the best part of eternity in exactly the same attire.

"If only we'd known."

Patrick licked his lips and Jason could tell that he was really getting to grips with his captive audience now and that—

"Yeah?" Patrick said, turning on Jason as if he had just shoved him in the back while the two of them had been participating in a soup queue. "And what *of* it?" From within the beaked head-dress of his costume, Patrick narrowed his eyes. "When it comes your turn, if you have to go through this, I'll bet your own Chan-neller will have to put up with the same, if not worse. So just indulge me a while, eh?"

For what seemed the millionth time, Jason reminded himself that everything which went on with the previously private confines of his skull, he might as well bark out—in his loudest voice—right into Patrick's ear. And as Jason did consider this form of action, Patrick—either hearing this thought of Jason's, or choosing to ignore it—swept merrily on from where he had left off.

"Once I met this guy all dressed up as a Tudor courtier. For some reason the guy wouldn't admit that he had been dressed up when he'd died—that he'd gone and overindulged himself on some stag-do and copped it; or else that he had been an employee at one of those Godforsaken, Medieval-themed fast-food restaurants."

Jason couldn't help but note Patrick's high-and-mighty tone, and he wondered if it was perhaps a trait shared among all Unquiet. As Jason well knew from his elders—blessed with experience—everything was *so much* easier in retrospect.

"I remember how he was constantly halting," Patrick contin-ued, "obviously rephrasing something in his mind so that it would sound more Thespian, or whatever."

Patrick paused for a moment.

"But little did he know that I can read minds, so imagine his surprise when I said, 'Listen, Clive, you're fooling nobody—everyone knows you're from Gowersbrudge and that you worked as a bank teller.' That seemed to get his attention, anyway, and, after that, he wasn't all 'high-and-mighty' about anything much at all."

Patrick shipped Jason a wink.

It took Jason a panicked second to divine the reason; that Patrick had read his mind and plucked that phrase out only moments before.

Patrick clapped his hands together. "All right, self-indulgence done with, why don't we have words about what we're going to do next, eh?"

"But you have not told us how you died."

Jason turned around, saw the blond girl was standing there.

He could hear a slight *twang* in her voice and, although he was no expert—the necessity for communication between humans would forever remain a mystery for Jason; and so modern languages, or ancient ones, for that matter, were well beyond Jason's capacity for comprehension—he was certain that she had a French accent.

He caught the blond-haired girl's gaze.

And she didn't look away instantaneously.

That *really was* a boon.

Wasn't it?

Patrick continued, replying to the blond girl, "Thought I'd go easy on you—spare you the details, but since you ask it seems rude not to give you some sort of explanation."

"It was a dark and foreboding night," Patrick intoned, in such a matter which suggested—to Jason, at least—that Patrick had rehearsed this speech to himself hundreds of times over.

Perhaps into a bathroom mirror.

"I had taken a good time in picking out my costume for the Christmas Eve Bash"—Patrick examined both Jason and the blond girl with a sidelong glance—"I know the name sounds somewhat corny to you two, but, trust me, at the time, it really was somewhat swell."

Patrick didn't go on with his story, and it seemed to breed a lingering disquiet among all three of them, standing on the bank of the canal.

Patrick stared hard first at the blond girl and then at Jason. "You gonna ask her what her name is, or what?"

"Huh?" Jason replied, rapid-fire, as was his wont.

Patrick rolled his eyes. "You just gonna go on referring to her as 'the blond girl' or are you gonna be a man and ask her what her real name is, huh?"

"Uh," Jason replied.

Clearly mocking Jason, Patrick opened his mouth so that it gaped wide. He glared out from within his chicken suit.

Although Jason was fairly certain he would've been well within his rights to feel outraged about this, he couldn't quite summon the strength.

"Go on," Patrick continued, shaking his head. "*You* ask her, or am I gonna have to do it?"

Jason's whole body—all his muscles—seized up tight.

For several moments, he couldn't breathe.

Like *not* at all.

A tingling sensation passed over the surface of his skin. His blood felt like it might freeze but this time it wasn't due to the outside temperature.

Nope, it was more like the feel of his own cowardice.

But then a very strange thing happened.

It was like something *snapped* inside him.

At the base of his ribcage.

Like something had been broken and could—never more— be repaired . . . but, for some reason, it felt like a *good* thing.

Jason really had no time at all to brief his brain—let alone his lips—on just what was going on here. Before he knew it, he blurted out, "I'm Jason—what's *your* name?"

Jason was operating on such a meet-and-greet high that he even found himself sticking out his hand for the blond girl to shake.

The blond girl—*quite understandably*—seemed somewhat taken aback by this sudden gesture.

But that distant grimace which'd previously dinged her features retreated slightly . . . and then, all at once, it was gone.

Perhaps for good.
Jason *hoped* for good.
She was giving him the approximation of a smile.
The *approximation* of a smile!
Hallelujah!

PLEASED TO MEET YOU

"*I* *am Fiona," the blond girl said.*

Jason almost missed *that* particular detail since he was concentrating so full-mindedly on the softness of her skin up against his.

Aside from his mother's skin, Jason really hadn't spent all that much time with female flesh and—if Jason was honest with himself—that was probably all the better for the theoretical females.

Now, though, the only way in which he could think to describe skin-on-skin was in all those clichés he had so often sneered at. The ones which'd crop up in everyday life from TV shows to programming manuals . . . the ones which were written in a chatty, everyday kind of style . . .

When Fiona finally slipped her dainty girl hand out away from Jason's crooked, aspiring programmer's fingers, he could hear a sort of low-level *hum* in his ears—almost possessing his mind with fury.

Jason had never quite felt this way before.

Not even when he had finally conquered a four-, or five-, hour debugging session and come away with a solution.

And—*my, oh my!*—those certainly had been highs.

This was totally different, though.

Perhaps it was the snow—maybe the freezing cold. Jason couldn't help but think that the current buzz he was experiencing was, by a distance, the most natural reaction he had ever had to *anything* in his entire life.

So this was Lurve—with a capital 'L' . . .

Fiona turned away from him. He was glad to notice that she didn't immediately replace her headphones—which now hung about her neck—up over her ears.

Was that a 'signal'?

Had all those 'terms' Jason overheard in communal eating areas, or the bus, in the library, pertained to some Real-World, tangible meaning?

Was this what people meant when they talked about an 'in' with a prospective romantic partner?

Jason couldn't think that it referred to anything else.

A silence opened up between the three of them—only the *whine* of the winter's wind, and the gentle *rustle* of snowflake on snowflake, served to break it.

When Jason glanced to Patrick, he saw that he was arching an eyebrow.

Jason finally caught the clue.

He turned to Fiona, who was staring, in a somewhat bored way, into the snow-covered canal beneath.

Jason made a conscious effort to keep his throat clear—to

avoid one of those embarrassing breakages in his voice. He had to make conversation somehow, and just about the only theme he could think to pick on was her accent. "Are you, uh, from *France?*"

Fiona at first didn't turn or react in any way to Jason.

Jason thought it might be due to the wind.

But she did finally turn.

Jason—thankfully—had no need to repeat himself.

Fiona looked at Jason with general beleaguerment.

She obviously had had various run-ins with British men in the past and—if her reaction to this latest barrage was anything to go by, those interactions really hadn't been anything to write home about: literally or metaphorically.

"Yes," she said, "Lion-sur-Mer."

"Oh," Jason replied, trying to think of anything at all that he might be able to say about Lion-sur-Mer, but, in the end, as usually happened, he came up short.

Thankfully, Patrick was standing by to at least thaw the uncomfortable silence which'd taken hold. "So," Patrick said, "my *death.*"

Both Jason and Fiona snapped back onto Patrick.

Patrick just gave them each a vague smile in recompense. "As I was saying, I was due to attend the much-celebrated Christmas Eve Bash at the *Fortnightly Arms*. Like always, I'd gone and had a little too much to drink before I so much as showed up at the place."

Patrick slanted his head to one side.

"Oh, just the odd drinkie here—the odd one *there*—no harm done. I never was one of those raving, lunatic drunks; the sort that tend to get into fist fights, and whoever knows what else . . .

but I did feel like I needed just a touch of Dutch courage that particular night because of what I had in mind."

Seeing an obvious opportunity for entering the discourse in a pain-free way, Jason said, "What did you have in mind?"

"Oh," Patrick said, in a flippant voice. "Nothing much *special* —just going to ask my boyfriend to marry me."

Jason observed Fiona slap her hands shut in a clasping, dreamy gesture.

Funny, Jason couldn't recall ever having seen anybody do that, outside of a film.

But he had now.

"A *proposal!*" Fiona said, in a voice which Jason decided was deeply alluring.

Jason found himself stumbling onto an altogether more surprising area. "Your boyfriend?"

Even to hear the words tumble out from between his lips was something of a surprise.

Of course Jason knew that men had sex with men, in theory—just as he knew that men had sex with women. All the same, it was something which crossed Jason's path so *infre-quently* in the Real World so as to be basically consigned to the same portion of his mind which pertained to unicorns and fairies.

Patrick rolled his eyes. "Oh, come *on*, you're not going to try and baptise me or something, are you?"

Not really understanding the question, but feeling that he should respond to it anyway, Jason said, "No, of course not."

"Good," Patrick continued, "because I could do without bigots as I wind up the thread which ties me to my final moments of existence."

Jason felt both his and Fiona's eyes glaze over at this particular statement.

"Anyway," Patrick continued, "there I was, all dressed up in my chicken suit and buzzing with the warmth and kindness and good will you'd be lucky to find in me twice in one lifetime, let alone on Christmas Eve."

"You were *drunk*?" Fiona put in.

Patrick met her with a glare, but his voice remained light. "I was most certainly *merry*." He drew breath and then continued. "While standing at the bus stop and waiting for a bus which would never come, due to the heavy snowfall, throughout town, and beyond, I felt a tiny skip enter my step."

Once more, Jason felt as if things were entering the realm of film and that there was very little he could do to prevent it.

Patrick shot Jason a pained glance.

Jason shut his brain up for good.

Patrick went on, "And when that damn, dusty regional 'express' failed to show, I looked out over the field and I asked myself 'Why not?'

"That night—*tonight*—I was determined that nothing was going to stand in my way.

"I had the silver-bound ring to ask after my sweetheart's hand in marriage. Things were all going to be so simple."

"But then you died," Fiona put in.

Jason found himself getting a little lost in the way that Fiona purred the 'th' of 'then', making it sound almost like a 'z'.

Patrick—understandably—turned a touch downbeat at this comment. "Yes, I waded my way across all those frozen fields, meandered through the backstreets, and slipped right down the bank of this *bloody* canal." He shook his head dejectedly.

"Screamed blue murder for a straight few minutes, too, but nobody came. And, like that"—Patrick snapped his fingers—"I went and froze to death."

Jason searched his mind for something—*anything*—he might be able to say to Patrick.

But he came up short.

Patrick sniffed a little, but Jason didn't notice so much as the glimmer of a tear in his eye.

Jason supposed that Patrick had had more than enough of basking in the memories of regret in his years of death—enough, certainly, to fill a lifetime, and then some . . .

There was a pregnant interlude and then, with a *hop* to his voice which didn't quite fit the sombre tone of what had come before, Patrick said, "All right, let's shove off, shall we?"

UNPLEASANT MEMORIES

P atrick *marched them off* away from the scene of his death. Jason was sincerely glad to be leaving it behind.

Although Jason knew so little of the Real World, he had already twigged that obsessing about the past really served no end whatsoever.

A life lesson learned, then . . .

As they plodded along through the snow drifts, Jason couldn't help his fantasies again taking hold. There was a certain something about the Spiritual Past which triggered his appetite in a great way—and, right now, he had an insane, unbridled desire for lentils.

With rice.

Was that such a strange desire?

As Jason wandered along in Patrick's wake, he wondered if their destination might feature an open-fire. Perhaps some festive—*glittering*—gold, silver and green decorations all sprinkled about.

Even though in Jason's own house his parents had never bothered to decorate, there was some weird, deeply ingrained sense that those things would bring about some kind of inner peace.

Or maybe Jason was just a human representation of the decades-long successes of marketing men.

They had—*somehow*—made him believe in something which simply wasn't there at all.

They trod onward through the increasingly packed snow until they emerged onto the main road of the town.

Here Jason did find his bearings, almost instantly.

Although much of the signage appeared somewhat dated, and where there had once been a charity shop there was now a butcher's, Jason recognised this as the main road through his university town.

It wasn't much, but it was—*kind of*—his.

Jason observed the garish, neon lights which hung from the shops:

A snowflake.

A holly leaf.

And then—much larger and spread across the entire width of the street from the second storey—a Santa driving a sleigh.

Jason hadn't been into town much after dark, and so it was reasonably surreal for him to be taking in these decorations for the first time. He wondered if it was like this every year. He wondered if it was like this *this* year . . . because, on his way to the bus station, he hadn't stopped for so much as a second to check.

Not even looked up from the scuffed toes of his shoes.

Patrick brought them to a halt soon after, at a whole bunch of steamed-up, perspiring windows.

Jason stood and stared at the façade.

He had been here before.

That was strange.

This was strange.

He observed the slick, shiny black paint which clung to the building. It looked like it had been freshly painted on . . . there were no parts where it had chipped away.

A pair of tinsel wreaths hung just inside the glass and a whole bunch of those electric-candle style lights flickered away in a somewhat festive fashion.

From within, Jason could hear the sound of bellowed Christmas Carols.

It *was* Christmas, after all.

Jason had come here in his first week of university.

Like most of his decisions, it had been ill-advised.

He had somehow got himself entangled in social discourse—some might've referred to it as a 'conversation'—with another boy from his computer-science course.

Said *boy* had managed to finagle it so that Jason walked along with him across campus, and little was Jason to know that they would end up where they did.

In a subsidiary hall.

It was there—in that fated subsidiary hall—that things rapidly got out of hand.

Before Jason knew it, there was a whole host of booths all spread out before him.

People wanting him to sign up for *things*.

Oh, the horror was so fresh in Jason's mind that he could still vividly recall the clubs—the *societies*—to which each belonged.

Volleyball.

Cricket.

Patchwork.

And *so* many more.

But it was Jason's impromptu companion who had brought them to their destination, to the booth which had clearly been ear-marked from the start.

Computer Club.

It had all happened so quickly.

One minute Jason had been this everyday, care-free, border-line sociopath . . . and then it had all changed.

Jason's companion—not to mention Jason himself—had signed up their names on some eager, grinning, red-haired boy's clipboard.

Jason had given him his *email*.

His *genuine* email.

Not even the one which he used to deflect spam.

To keep himself free of unsolicited correspondence.

And that had been a condemnation, in a way.

Jason had been roped into the 'initiation' ceremony. And this had entailed them all taking the bus, arriving in town, and then walking along to where they had arrived just this moment.

To where Jason stood with Patrick and Fiona right now.

The Fortnightly Arms.

"You all right there, pal?" Patrick said. "Look like you've seen a ghost."

Jason felt his whole body tingling at the realisation of what this place meant to him.

They had gone in—just over a dozen of them, all male, of course—and Jason recalled all the boys cajoling him—*cajoling him!*—into drinking pint after pint of *beer*.

There had seemed no end!

And all the time, they had intoned something which they referred to as the *Programmers' Paradigm*, and which—aside from its technical-sounding name—had been an extremely lewd lyrical phrase and had clearly bothered other customers of the establishment.

Other customers at the *pub*.

Jason had barely escaped with his life.

He could still vividly recall babbling to the others that he was going to the toilet, only for him to slip out the back door of the pub.

Head spinning, and nausea creeping over him, Jason had zigzagged his way back up the street still tasting the sour flavour of 'ale' scarring his tonsils and the wider area which represented the back of his throat.

He remembered the stink of disinfectant—all around—the stuff the night-time cleaners had splashed just about everywhere around the city centre.

And with good reason.

All the same, Jason had almost felt like he could hear the disinfectant sloshing about beneath his feet . . . although it *hadn't* been . . . of course, it hadn't been.

Then he had caught the bus home and spent much of the rest of the night—and a great deal of the next morning—vomiting into a toilet.

Jason hadn't drunk since.

Not *alcohol*, in any case.

Jason felt Patrick's hand on his shoulder.

He noticed Fiona was observing him with some concern.

That was good, wasn't it?

"I'm fine," Jason said, feeling even more white-faced than he had previously.

Without saying a word, but smiling all over the shop, Patrick clapped Jason on the shoulder and led them all inside the *The Fortnightly Arms*.

THE FORTNIGHTLY ARMS

J*ason would've liked* to say the pub was just as he
remembered it

But there was the matter that Jason recalled nothing of
the ill-fated 'Computer Club' night.

He supposed that the one bonus of this particular pub was
that it appeared identical—or *near enough*—to every single pub
that Jason might've imagined.

This was to say that there was a walnut-toned bar. One of
those brass railings trimming it—were those things meant to
help give drunks swaying on their barstools some much-needed
stability when they required it?

Behind the bar were the assorted bottles of liquor—or *was* it
liquor?—which Jason wouldn't have been able to identify even
with some sort of an alcoholic drinks encyclopaedia to hand.

Jason shuddered at just the thought of the existence of such
a book . . .

The air smelled—as the air in bars always did—of sour, spilled beer.

Then there was that odour of vomit hastily covered-up with sawdust, and then spiked with disinfectant.

It all caught at the back of his throat.

And wouldn't—under any circumstances—let go.

Although Jason was really no expert on pubs—to put it mildly—he thought the décor looked a touch sun-faded; the once-rich, turquoise-green barstool cloth now closer to a dusty lime.

But Patrick seemed happy enough.

In his chicken costume, he strutted up to the pumps, consulted with the bored-looking barman, who had a thick, black handlebar moustache and—the barman giving Jason and Fiona a quick once-over—he commenced to pour out three pints of ale.

As the barman poured the pints, Fiona tapped Patrick on his shoulder and Jason overheard her say something about wanting a 'gin and tonic'.

Patrick shook his head in reply, with an easy smile.

Jason overheard the response, "Nah, love, you're on my time —and that means getting a proper drink down you."

Jason really had next to no idea what a 'proper' drink entailed. If rushed to describe it for himself, he might've said something along the lines of a 'glass of tap water'.

But that wasn't very 'rock and/or roll'.

With the pints poured, Patrick led Fiona over to a small nook. It consisted of a wooden corner bench with appropriate cushions. 'Appropriate cushions' didn't mean there was something offensive about them, but that, with their battered, turtle-shell brown shade, they seemed to match the rest of the pub quite nicely.

As Jason sat down, he noticed the Christmas tree which stood in the corner of the pub, and which had been decorated with thin streamers of silver and gold.

Matching lights.

There was a dainty—most likely—hand-crafted star perched on top.

Although Jason had long thought himself immune to all such crap, he couldn't help but feel a slight skip in his heart at the sight.

Maybe he was going all soppy at last.

Perhaps—finally—sentimentality had paid him a visit.

Or it might've just been that Jason had gas.

That was always a possibility . . .

The three of them all sat down at the table—*circular*—each of them perched on a bit of bench cushion. Jason was close enough to Fiona that, if he'd had the guts, and been fairly confident such an act wouldn't be met with a blood-curdling scream, he could have reached out to touch her hand beneath the table.

Which was a long-winded way of saying that Jason was sitting *beside* Fiona . . . in fact, he was sandwiched between Fiona *and* Patrick.

For the first time in their acquaintance, Jason noted that Patrick had gone quiet.

Patrick had supped at the foamy, slightly caramel-coloured head of his beer, but hadn't touched it aside from that. He was staring off wistfully into the middle distance as if he—*himself*—was seeing a ghost.

Perhaps—one way or another—*all* of them were seeing ghosts.

That just seemed the way things were going these days.

Jason knew, in his role as Channeller, that it was up to him to work out how to get his Unquiet what he wanted.

But, for some reason, Jason could see no way of aiding him.

They were here.

Right where Patrick had wanted to be.

All they needed to do was wait for Patrick's soon-to-be betrothed to show his face, and the job would be a Good 'Un.

But sitting at the circular table in his chicken suit, it was hard to deny that Patrick looked somewhat down.

Even for Jason, who had the social skills of a lamppost.

Jason decided that—really—he should step in. So he put in a tentative, "Uh, is everything okay?"

Patrick remained still.

His eyes within the beaked head of the costume turned their focus down onto the honey-coloured liquid of his ale, as if he could see things in that ale which—even with years of study—Jason would never be able to see.

Patrick gave a hardy smile in profile. "Just wondered if this is the right thing to do, mate."

Jason very consciously *didn't* think of anything at all.

He wasn't going to fall for *that* old party trick.

Not again . . .

As Jason prepared his response, he shifted his glance over to Fiona, seeing that she was inspecting him closely—clearly waiting to see what wisdom Jason might impart.

Patrick's smile cracked wider. "Wouldn't call it 'wisdom', mate."

Bugger.

That mind trick again . . .

Well, Jason was just going to have to go for it.

"I'd say so, mate," Patrick replied.

"Look," Jason said, "could you just stop reading my mind for one second? I'm trying to help you."

Patrick forced his smile into a sort of grimace. "Wish it was that easy, mate. It's kinda like trying to have a conversation with the TV blaring off some nonsense or other."

From somewhere around them, Jason heard a few waves of static.

And then—again, from *somewhere*—he heard the first few beats to what was, even to Jason's untrained ear, a gay-sounding song.

Patrick's expression immediately brightened. He smiled a broad grin and took a hefty draught of his ale. And then—with no explanation; no *attempt* at an explanation—he grabbed both Jason and Fiona by the hand and hurtled them to their feet.

Before Jason really knew what'd happened, he was standing on the dancefloor.

Uh, oh, this couldn't end well . . .

THE DANCEFLOOR

F or *Jason*, at least, it was a seriously surreal situation. And, of all the surreal situations which'd occurred in—What even *was* the time frame? . . . Was it still Christmas Eve?—this was quite probably the one which broke the proverbial camel's back.

There was still nobody else in the pub.

Just the handlebar-moustached barman who was currently polishing a pint glass with a grease-spotted, once-white tea towel.

Jason could tell—although he couldn't *quite* make out the full resolution of his features in the gloom—that the barman was smiling to himself.

And why *shouldn't* he be?

He *was* observing what very well might've been The Funniest Sight in his Life, which—to put it more precisely—was Jason dancing.

Or attempting to.

The impromptu dancefloor took the form of a sticky patch of linoleum right beneath a cluster of leaves and berries hanging from the ceiling.

It was as Jason considered this *odd* collection of leaves and berries that he found his thought process—a little abruptly —cut off.

Patrick leaned into him, grasped the back of his head and thrust his lips up against his own.

To say Jason was alarmed was perhaps an understatement.

He had never once *considered* the possibility of kissing another man.

. . . But, then again, he had never *seriously* considered that he would ever really get the opportunity to kiss a *woman*, so—in the moment—he did his best to pick up any sort of tips that might be useful for later.

However, before the kiss had truly begun, it was all over.

Patrick's bristly mouth—not to mention the rather surreal aspect of it being framed by a foam chicken beak—retreated from Jason's.

Patrick was glancing upward.

To the cluster of leaves and berries which hung above their heads.

"Mistletoe," Patrick said, in a gruff voice.

When Jason looked in Fiona's direction, he realised she was smiling.

Jason felt a flash of embarrassment pass through his chest, but, before he could *really* narrow it down, Patrick whispered— into Jason's mind; just as Old Mother Time had done:

— *Go on, my son. Give her a corker. Right on the kisser, eh?*

Strangely—although it seemed as if Patrick might be speaking a totally different language—Jason seemed to understand without too much effort at all.

It was almost like that time he'd been to France on a school trip and—though the purpose of the trip had been for them to practise their rudimentary, foreign-language skills—Jason hadn't been able to say anything beyond a wavering 'bonjour'.

He hadn't even been able to gather enough resolve to try out speaking to the natives in *English*.

And so he had been reduced to hand gestures.

Kind of like a toddler.

Or a monkey . . .

But when he had spotted this seashell, or some other trinket, he had managed to communicate exactly what he wished using only gestures and vague noises from the back of his throat.

And that was the sort of understanding that Jason was operating on right now.

He looked to Fiona, who—a little vacantly—looked right back at him.

Through the unseen speakers, music continued to pour.

All that cranking bass and endlessly catchy melody.

Jason knew—just thinking about it—that the song would remain lodged in his brain for weeks.

In their triangle, they all continued to put together some sort of mechanical chain of dance moves.

If ever there would be a moment then this was it.

As Jason sort of thought about leaning in for a kiss with Fiona beneath the mistletoe, a cry—from the base of Patrick's lungs—rang out . . . even over the too-loud, insanely catchy music.

Patrick reached out, grabbed a hold of the sleeve of Jason's hoodie and dragged him on across the dancefloor.

Opportunity: Blown.

When Jason caught a glance back over his shoulder, he saw that Fiona was nonchalantly following on their heels. Apparently she didn't wish to dance on her own, and—Jason for one—didn't blame her.

"Sorry to break up the romance, pal!" Patrick barked—or should that have been *crowed?*—in Jason's ear. "But you've gotta meet my friend, Eric."

" 'Eric'?" Jason replied, a little beleaguered.

But Patrick only clapped Jason on the shoulder in reply.

Eric turned out to be a man, in perhaps his forties, entirely dressed in ladies' underwear.

The *really* lacy kind.

Eric had a bald head and a thriving red beard which sort of burst out of his cheeks the same way that lava spews forth from the crater of a volcano. He had on a pearl necklace. His eyes—and lips—were heavily made up.

Jason didn't have much of a clue about how to deal with this meeting, but—*luckily*—Patrick was very much on hand to help him out.

"Eric, Jason—Jason, Eric."

An exchange of dour nods, then Patrick performed the same feat with Fiona, who struck a sheepish stance at Jason and Patrick's heels.

Before Jason could really square what'd just happened, Eric

reached out and thumped him in the chest. In a way which could've generously been described as 'playful'.

"Whatcha drinkin' then, sunshine?"

"Uh," Jason replied, thoroughly stumped by the dual onslaught of having to recover breath *and* think of some drink that wouldn't immediately mark him out as a rank amateur.

Jason vaguely pointed off in the direction of the table where their drinks still stood. "Same again?" he said, hopefully.

Eric, in all his lingerie glory, gave a brisk nod and then set off across the floor of the pub at a determined pace.

Jason found himself staring right into the beak of the chicken once again.

Glaring right into Patrick's *expectant* eyes. "You think we could have a word, pal?"

Recalling his role as Channeller—though how Jason had ever allowed himself to forget truly escaped him—Jason gave a nod and, together with Patrick, he wandered back over in the direction of the table where they'd previously been sat.

When they did sit down, Jason, keeping his voice low, even, said, "Where's Fiona gone?"

Patrick jerked his thumb over his shoulder to indicate some darkened interior doorway of the pub. "Gone off to the ladies, hasn't she." And here Patrick gave Jason a slight smile. "Off to powder her nose."

After this quip, Patrick's manner became more introspective . . . which was to say that he shifted the focus of his gaze to the glass of ale sitting on the table before him. "Wanted to think out loud to myself," Patrick continued. "For what it's worth."

Jason kept his brain as prim and alert as he could manage.

He wanted to help out his assigned Unquiet to the very best of his ability.

"It's just, you get thinking, you know, you think you've gone and got something sussed out—a sort of issue that's been standing in your way since Time Immemorial, and then up spring the doubts, up come all these extra things that you never really thought about at all."

" 'Doubts'?" Jason repeated.

Patrick flashed his eyebrows. "Yeah."

Patrick seemed to drift off for another few moments, lost to his own thoughts . . . in his own world, then he went on, "Anyway, back when I decided, before I *died*"—he seemed to apply a certain gravity to the word as it so demanded—"I'd been turning over just what'd go on if I asked my boyfriend to marry me."

Seeing an 'in' for this conversation—something which might indicate his unshaking interest—Jason asked, "What was your boyfriend's name, again?"

At this, Patrick gave a slight smile.

One of those *most natural* of smiles; the ones which veritably *burst* off the lips.

"Andrew," Patrick replied, finally.

Patrick seemed to lose himself in the amber liquid within his glass then he continued from where he'd left off. "Anyway, thing is that I'd been thinking all about the idea of us getting married —scoping out all the angles."

He paused briefly, clutched his glass for a few seconds, appearing to think about drinking, then to think better of it.

Finally, he released the glass.

Jason was very aware of his own glass of ale. More for the fact that he hadn't taken so much as a sip for several minutes.

And so—reluctant—Jason brought the cool glass up to his lips and sipped at the bitter, stinking-socks tasting—and *smelling*—liquid from within.

When Jason set his glass down, he neatly convinced himself that he could actually *hear* the grim *slosh* of the ale making its way through his digestional tract.

Patrick was grinning again. "Good stuff that—puts hair on your chest, no doubt."

But, as Patrick went on with his story, Jason couldn't quite pin down exactly what Patrick had meant.

Jason already had a pretty bushy chest already, thank you very much.

FEELINGS AND STUFF

Although *Jason* often found that his brain flipped onto Standby when somebody got deeply down into the nitty-gritty of their life details, he actually managed to keep himself at least *looking* marginally interested.

Still tasting the stinking socks at the back of his throat, Jason noticed—out of the corner of his eye—that Fiona had returned from the bathroom.

Fresh from 'powdering her nose', whatever *that* meant.

Patrick's story, as far as Jason absorbed it, was one fraught with jealousy, inner-conflict and—*strangely*—speculative, aesthetic dental work.

This was the matter which Patrick had used as the latest catalyst to spark fresh doubts about his relationship with Andrew.

Patrick rested his elbows on the table and, as he spoke, he addressed his—now-empty—pint glass sitting before him.

"It was just another one of those communication breakdowns."

Patrick, as he'd revealed a little earlier, had been a therapist and he was very keen, Jason had observed, on labelling particular parts of his relationship with Andrew.

"A silly thing, really," Patrick went on. "I've never felt right about my teeth, not one jot, really. And, well, you'll see later, Andrew has just got himself born with this *perfect* set"—Patrick paused for a moment's thought—"this *near* perfect set, anyway."

Jason tried to have some sort of a point of view—positive or negative about Patrick's teeth—but he really could see nothing at all wrong with them. Then again, Jason had always just seen teeth as a sort of awkward evolutionary trade-off . . . an impro-vised solution so that food might be swallowed.

Patrick steeped himself in silence for a long few seconds.

Jason couldn't help feeling concerned that he might've read his thoughts and be preparing some sort of a counter-attack.

As it was, though, Patrick just continued as he had before.

"Guess it goes back to school, really," Patrick went on, "weird thing, but the only name the kids gave me that got to me—that *really* got to me—was *Fang*."

" 'Fang'?" Jason repeated, momentarily distracted as Fiona descended into her seat.

"Mm," Patrick said, and went on staring at his empty glass.

It was at this point that some sort of pub etiquette seemed to sink into Jason's skin.

Somewhere in the deeper recesses of Jason's mind, he got the urge to ask Patrick if he would like another drink.

And, as it happened, Patrick did.

"Cheers, pal," Patrick said.

Feeling just a touch jittery on his feet—Jason had never ordered a drink in a pub before; back at that Computer Club social gathering, some other boy had done all the ordering—he trod over the creaking floorboards and up to the brass railing of the bar.

The man with the handlebar moustache was still wiping clean the same glass he had been cleaning since they came in.

When it came right down to it, all glasses looked fairly similar . . .

The barman gave Jason nothing much more than a vague incline of the head to indicate he was receptive to receiving an order.

And Jason wasn't in any sort of mood to waste time.

"Um," Jason began—unconvincingly. "An ale, and"—here Jason made a point of lowering his tone so that he wouldn't be overheard by either Fiona or Patrick, sitting over at their table in the corner—"do you have anything that, erm, you know, sort of stops you from getting drunk?"

The barman screwed up his expression.

Wrinkles formed in his brow.

Jason clearly had gone and said something mind-numbingly stupid.

No taking it back now, though.

The barman finally responded. "You mean, like a non-alcoholic beer?" As he finished up this statement, he stooped down to a mini fridge on the other side of the bar and removed a light-green bottle from within. He laid it down on the walnut bar counter with a slight *clink* and then stood back to await Jason's reaction.

"Uh," Jason said, "sure, and does that have something inside of it that makes you"—Jason scoured his brain for the correct nomenclature—"sober?"

This only brought out yet more consternation from the barman.

And Jason couldn't help but get the feeling—despite his social afflictions—that he was very much getting on the barman's nerves.

"Dunno what you're talking 'bout, mate. This is a *pub*, yeah? People come here to get drunk, capiche?"

Though Jason didn't speak Italian—was that Italian?—he understood enough from the context to know what the barman was attempting to communicate.

It was all in his eyes.

In his *extremely angry* eyes . . .

"So," the barman said, through bared teeth. "What'll it be?"

And then, as Jason finally settled on the decision that he *would* go for the non-alcoholic beer, he realised he had misplaced his wallet.

When he informed the barman it was fair to say he wasn't best pleased.

They returned to the table with Patrick's wallet a little lighter. Patrick had claimed that money really didn't matter; first, because this was the Spiritual Past; and, second, because, very soon—all being well—Patrick would be travelling to the Everafter.

If Patrick was sure of anything at all, he was certain that

there would be no such broad concept as 'money' to be dealt with.

"So," Patrick said, his voice with a slightly playful jolt to it, "you got any sort of great advice—oh, my chosen spiritual advisor?"

Jason gave a wry smile in return, his sarcasm detector apparently very much in functioning order.

"Seriously, though, pal," Patrick continued, "you're on the clock—so to speak—any sort of guidance you'd like to give would be *much* appreciated."

And although Jason would've very much liked to give his advice—his *opinion*—on the current state of matters, as they related to Patrick and his boyfriend; his attention was caught by a sharp motion out of the corner of his eye.

Fiona.

She was . . . well, looking around extremely rapidly, almost as if she was *hyper* in some way.

She reminded Jason of when he had worked one summer at the corner shop near his house. Every day—without fail—a woman of about forty, Jason supposed, would turn up in the shop with her children who would instantly commence rifling through the Pick 'n' Mix cabinets—each of them filling up one of the paper bags until they, more often than not, gathered together something like a kilo of sweets each.

As their mother would pay for the Pick 'n' Mix which, to Jason, had always seemed to be priced scandalously, the children would munch their way through their respective bags.

The transformation was instantaneous.

It always was.

First it would be as simple as a sparkle in the eye—almost as if the sugar had somehow crystallised and appeared on the surface of their eyeballs . . . yeah, something like that.

Next would come the jittery reactions.

The *tweaker* motions.

Neither of the children—even as the embattled mother handed over the cash—would be physiologically capable of standing still.

They would *hum* about like . . . like *bees*.

And then the true carnage would begin.

One or another of the children would dash off—perhaps taking down a display which Jason had lovingly crafted during the course of a brutally boring morning.

The mother, and every day it got fainter and fainter, would tell off one or both children to no discernible result.

Every day would be the same.

The mother trudging on the heels of her offspring would half turn to Jason at the counter, mumbling apologies to him as if the same thing wouldn't happen the following day.

Or the day after that.

The day after *that*.

What brought those children to mind was the way Fiona was all perked up, just like she was on a sugar high.

As Fiona leaped to her feet—clearly about to cause untold chaos—Jason acted on gut instinct, doing what he had non-verbally *commanded* the mother of those children to do *every single afternoon*.

Perhaps Jason should've written her a note and left it surreptitiously on the counter for her to read . . . yeah, and pigs might've *flown*.

Jason grabbed Fiona's wrist.

It was far—*far*—more delicate than Jason could ever have imagined.

What happened next was so sudden, so *beyond* the realm of Jason's capacity for reading the situation, that he was taken off guard completely.

Fiona drew back the fist of her other arm—the one which *didn't* pertain to the wrist Jason clasped tightly—and she laid a bunch of fives smack right on the bridge of Jason's nose.

Later on, as Jason pieced together the testament of witnesses —the barman; Patrick—he would hear about how there had been an almighty *crack*!

All that Jason really knew at that point, though, was that the world got awfully *spinny*.

And then awfully black.

KNOCKOUT!

J*ason felt like* there was somebody sticking hot pins all around his nose and mouth.

He could feel his heart hammering right at the back of his tonsils.

When he breathed in, all he could smell was that rancid odour of stinking socks—*ale* . . . and there was the taste of blood to contend with too.

Through the bells which rang about Jason's hearing, he could hear voices.

Gentle.

Indistinct.

But, then again, Jason had never really been much of an expert when he listened to them—at least when it came to *identifying* said voices.

Maybe he just needed to try harder, or something.

Gradually, Jason became aware of the sturdy hands, all of

them gripping him, helping him back up to his feet. And although Jason really wasn't the biggest fan of skin-on-skin contact in the world, he did tolerate it . . . if only because he couldn't see straight.

The world just went *spin-spin-spin* before his very eyes.

Jason cracked one eye open—and then the other.

At first, he was only looking at blurs.

Indistinct—but colourful—shapes.

They made noises too.

Jason analysed the various shapes before him and soon identified the bright-yellow blur.

Patrick.

The man in the chicken suit.

A little way back from him—Jason might've said a *polite* distance back—was Fiona.

The one who'd—*briefly*—rendered Jason unconscious and in dire need of manly assistance to regain his former posture.

Soon enough, Jason found himself staring hard at Fiona.

Maybe it was the concussion speaking—in all probability it was—but Jason's former timidity suddenly deserted him.

Never to be found again?

Or just disappeared on a brief holiday?

Jason rubbed his temple and did his best to straighten out his vision.

He wasn't one-hundred-per-cent successful.

But he was successful *enough*.

"You," Jason began, feeling the word shake through him strongly enough that it had—surely—taken his target off guard. "Why'd you do that?"

Jason swayed for several heart-stopping seconds before refinding his balance.

"Why'd you *hit* me?"

Fiona was rendered speechless. Her eyeballs were rolling all over the shop.

Jason wasn't sure what she would do.

If she would return to finish the job she'd started.

Once more, Jason's mind flexed over to that very basic question of whether or not one could die within the Spiritual Past.

Jason really had very little interest in putting the matter to a practical trial so that he might have an answer one way or another.

As Jason formulated a further opening line to an interrogation, his sense—and timid personality returning—Fiona's eyes widened.

Then she promptly turned on her heel.

And ran.

Jason really had very little clue about just what he was doing before he felt the chilly night air sting his cheeks.

When he peered out before himself, keeping his focus very much fixed on the escaping Fiona, he could see snowflakes drifting down—ever so slowly—to the icy pavements below.

And though Jason was *certain* he was going to slip and fall flat on his arse at any second, he managed to defy the laws of physics and remain—pretty much—on his two feet.

Hell, he actually managed to *catch* Fiona.

The way it happened, Jason would probably have freely

admitted out loud, was something like a bad, late-night action movie.

Fiona bolted on down a side alley—clearly hoping; nay, *praying*—that it might offer a free escape.

Alas, it was a dead-end.

And Jason found himself boxing the flittish Fiona right at the end of it.

Even in the dim, orange streetlights with the snowflakes meandering downward, Jason could make out the reddish colour which'd entered Fiona's cheeks.

The way her eyes had gone all black.

She had nowhere to run.

And Jason had her all alone.

All to himself.

As he took a step forward,, he wondered just what he was going to do. Before he could take another, he needed not ask himself any further questions.

"Stop," Fiona said.

Jason did.

Fiona looked pale in the moonlight which shone on down through the clouds, illuminating her features . . . and Jason couldn't help thinking that she looked—*really*—quite beautiful.

Sexy.

And then Jason noticed the little dribble of snot hanging down from her left nostril.

Fiona fixed Jason with her gaze. Her eyes were wide and— probably, if Jason had been able to see their level of detail in the night light—webbed with red veins.

"I am sorry," Fiona said, pronouncing the last syllable as if it carried all the stress of the world.

Jason really had no idea how to respond.

It had sounded genuinely *heartfelt* . . . but, then again, she *had* punched him in the face.

Fiona stared deeply into Jason's eyes and then turned her focus downward, to the tips of her shoes. "You have no idea."

"No idea about what?" Jason said, sounding much spikier than he had planned to.

His nose *did* really smart . . .

"You have no idea what it means—what it *really* means—to be dead."

Jason allowed this accusation to tumble about his mind for several seconds and then responded, "You're probably right."

Fiona continued to stare downward as if some utterly compelling pantomime was taking place there . . . all right not a *pantomime*; something *entertaining* . . .

"When it happened"—suddenly, unexpectedly, Fiona looked up at Jason, meeting his eye—"when I *died*, I did not know at all what I should expect."

Jason felt a flash of pain throb through his nose. He reached up and gave it a reassuring stroke with his fingers, and then, tasting the blood at the back of his throat, tried not to wonder when his capacity for smell might return.

And perhaps it was these particular thoughts which led Jason to throw in just a little snarky twist into his reply. "What? Expected singing angels? Blaring trumpets?"

All right, *a lot* of snark.

Fiona looked a little bemused at this comment for several seconds, and then, blinking once—*twice*—seemed to get over her confusion. She even managed to raise a faint smile.

Maybe she was under some illusion that Jason was trying out some of his famous *British* wit on her.

. . . If only she knew the truth.

"No," Fiona said, replying in an even voice, "but I was not expecting there to be nothing to happen."

" 'Nothing'?" Jason replied, scaling back the snark consciously.

Fiona nodded. "*Nothing.*"

It was here that Fiona added an—admittedly well-placed —sigh.

Then she continued.

"When I died, and nothing at all happened, it was like I was still alive. I continued to walk around, much like you and I do now. I could still *hear*. I could still *see*. And *touch*. And *taste*. *Smell* the world which surrounded me . . . and yet . . . and yet, I felt like I was separate; that it was holding me at a, uh . . . uh . . ."

"Arm's length?" Jason put in, wanting to help her out.

Fiona grinned back at him. "Yes," an 'arm's length'."

The idiom sounded somewhat unconvincing leaking out through her lips.

Fiona put her game face back on. "It was impossible to deal with my new reality—for me to be both *here*, and *not here*, able to interact with my surroundings but to have no impact on them whatsoever."

Jason felt like he was putting together the pieces, though he would've been extremely reluctant to admit as much out loud.

"And so I began to take cocaine."

Jason couldn't say with any certainty that he had ever known a drug addict, or, for that matter, anybody he knew for sure had even *taken* drugs.

And yet, he acknowledged that it must go on.

That—apparently unbeknownst to Jason—all these 'good times' were going on.

"It helped me," Fiona went on, "it made me feel a little more balanced."

" 'Balanced'? In what way?"

"Oh," Fiona replied, in that care-free, French-girl way of hers, "just something to do before I leave this place forever."

"Which place?"

"The world."

"Oh, yeah," Jason replied, "*that* place . . . I've heard *all about* that place." And right then Jason felt a smile break out over his lips.

He couldn't help himself.

Fiona smiled back.

"You think we should go see what Patrick is up to? This is *his* Spiritual Past, after all . . ."

BACK TO THE SPIRITUAL PAST

The pub—compared with how it had been before—was totally transformed.

Gone was the creeping sense of solitude which clung to the place.

It had been replaced by a bristling multitude.

Ton upon ton of men in fancy dress.

Jason hardly had time to register them all in the sensory upheaval—from the quiet, empty streets of the town to this bubbling room of energy.

He observed a man with his hair dyed a bright pink, another dressed up as a biker—or perhaps he was an *actual* biker?—then there was the incredibly distinctive man wearing a silky, light-purple dress.

And carrying a glittery, silver wand.

To say that Jason really had no idea what to make of this spectacle would be to put the matter very lightly indeed. Thankfully, Fiona grabbed Jason by his elbow, and that acted as a kind of calming effect on him.

His heartrate slowed.

It was easier for him to accept his surroundings.

The hordes and hordes of people attending the Christmas Eve Bash.

Jason was attempting to identify Patrick.

But, it seemed, he was nowhere to be found.

Although Fiona continued to drag Jason along through the— apparently never-ending—crowd, Jason felt something, deep inside, imploring him to head for the toilets.

For some reason, the toilets were where he needed to be . . . though he didn't think to question this particular instinct *too* closely.

Jason succeeded in slipping free of Fiona's vicelike grasp on his arm. He felt his skin pinch just a little beneath her touch. But, before Fiona could grab hold of Jason once more, he was gone.

He had escaped.

Jason remained focussed, feeling the gentle—natural?—*creak* of the wooden floorboards beneath his weight. It took near enough all Jason's concentration to worm his way through the men all packed together and, without exception, outfitted in fancy dress.

The toilets were marked out by some graffitied wooden panels. One of a crudely drawn penis, and another of a similarly —Jason *assumed*—crudely drawn vagina.

Jason made the jump of logic which sent him off in the direction of the men's.

The toilets—just like *all* public toilets—were done up with white porcelain.

The air stank of urinal cake and piss and—much to Jason's disgust—*faeces*.

Right away—and perhaps this was his Channeller instinct kicking in because it *certainly* wasn't his normal mind—Jason noted that one of the cubicle doors was shut tight.

And that sobbing emanated from within.

Bingo.

Jason sidled up to the door and clunked his knuckles against it in what—he hoped—would be interpreted as a knock.

The sobbing ceased.

Jason wondered if he had his 'in'.

He decided to push the boat out.

"Patrick?" he said. "Is that you in there?"

A long pause on the other side of the door, but a rogue *sniffle* eventually gave Patrick away.

"Leave me alone," Patrick said, his voice echoing around the otherwise vacated toilets.

Jason wondered if Fiona would join them shortly or if she had decided to go do the 'social' thing and mingle.

This was *none* of her problem, after all.

She had only been assigned to Jason so that there might be some sort of a romantic angle to be played . . . or—*at least*—that'd been Jason's interpretation.

Was he *really* that horny?

"You're so *self-absorbed*," came Patrick's voice from within the cubicle, "you're meant to be helping me out—trying to fix what went wrong in *my* life; give me a satisfying ending, and the only thing you can think about is *breeding*."

Oh, yeah, Jason had gone and forgotten—*for the millionth time* —that his thoughts were all fair game for Patrick.

But Patrick seemed to get over this slight—if that was how he interpreted it—almost instantly. "It's just," Patrick continued, as if nothing at all had happened, "I don't know if this is the right thing to do."

Still feeling a touch numb following the *impromptu* mind-reading trick, Jason could only repeat—zombie-like—" 'The right thing'."

"Yeah, pal," Patrick continued, as if Jason might be any use whatsoever with a relationship dilemma. "I'm not sure this is how I want to go out—if you see what I mean?"

"You don't want to propose marriage to Andrew?"

"Is that so bad?"

"Which one is Andrew?"

A short pause on Patrick's end of the conversation, and then, "He's the one wearing the dress."

Jason stretched his mind.

But not too far.

"He's, uh"—Jason started to think about how to express something positive in a non-gay way but then he reminded himself that Patrick was party to all his thoughts—"Quite *dashing*," Jason finally settled on.

When Patrick spoke again, Jason could hear the smile in his voice. "He is, isn't he, pal?"

From within the toilet, Jason heard Patrick give an—apparently—long-held sigh, and then, with a slight puff of air, the flushing mechanism of the toilet sounded.

Maybe it was the ale but Jason suddenly felt like his mind

was occupied with twirling whirlpools, flushing downward in ever-faster spins.

Another sigh emanated from within the toilet cubicle, and then, "Well, pal, I guess I've no choice, have I?"

Jason held his counsel.

The lock on the cubicle door slid back with a sharp *click*. The tiny laminated plastic sign which'd previously read 'Occupied', in a danger *red*, was replaced by 'Vacant' written against an all-stations-go *green*.

Patrick emerged from within the toilet. He clutched, in his left hand, down at his side, a small, patterned green box with a ribbon tied about it. "This feels like a massive mistake." He drew in a breath and then exhaled hard. "But, whatever, huh?"

Even to Jason—who wasn't remotely romantically inclined, to put it mildly—the whole scene unfolding *did* touch him. In a way.

Perhaps, looking at the thing from an egotistical angle, Jason was glad *he* had been the one involved in the final 'pep' talk.

The one who'd finally driven Patrick over the edge . . . so to speak.

Whatever the reason, Jason found himself smiling as he observed Patrick getting down on one knee. The crowd encir-cling him.

Getting the deed done.

It was just as Jason met Fiona's eye when he felt the world retreating.

He could feel the darkness washing over him.

Beckoning him inside.

And then he was back.

But not without Andrew's final, sustained, "*Yes!*" echoing about his skull.

A SATISFYING CONCLUSION?

The details returned to Jason gradually. The first thing which really *struck* him was how the bone-quakingly cold temperature shook him right down to his core elements. He breathed in the smell of disinfectant. The— now slightly haunting—Christmas music clicked and crackled out of the knackered waiting room speakers. And then Jason felt the hard-backed, heavy wooden bench return beneath him.

When he finally opened his eyes, he was somewhat disappointed to still have the stinky-sock taste of ale filling his mouth.

The only ones within the bus-station waiting room now were Jason, Fiona and Old Mother Time.

Everybody else had gone home.

Jason had *got* them all home.

But he tried not to let that fact go to his head.

On instinct, Jason looked off in the direction of Old Mother Time.

She was asleep.

Unflinching.

Undisturbed.

So Jason took his chances and flashed a glance over at Fiona.

She stared right back at him.

Smiled slightly.

A warmth flowed up from the pit of Jason's chest and—for a heart-stopping moment—he was certain that he was going to vomit.

But he didn't . . .

Was this love?

Was this Lurve, with a capital 'L'?

It merited further investigation.

And so, doing something which he never—*ever*—would've dreamed of doing before he had entered the bus-station waiting room that evening, he left his bulky, travel computer rucksack behind and approached Fiona.

She said nothing as he took the final steps toward her.

As he loomed right above her.

They stood like that, pinned to that particular moment in time—Jason's time—and exchanged glances.

Although Jason couldn't be totally certain, he was fairly sure that what he was doing could have been termed 'losing' himself in her eyes.

When Jason spoke, his own voice startled him.

It was so firm.

So *assured*.

He wondered if it had been him at all who had spoken.

But, when he glanced over to Old Mother Time, he saw that she slept on.

Was there any rule that psychics—if that was what Old Mother Time was—couldn't perform mind-reading tricks if they were sleeping?

All the same, Jason did say, "I'd like to help you, with your death—if you'll allow me."

Fiona stared back into his eyes and said, "Don't you mean my *life?*"

And, in that particular context, it didn't sound that *schmoozy* at all . . .

Jason felt the whole world coming apart once again.

Or, perhaps more accurately, *falling apart*, only for it to rebuild itself the very next instant.

When the world did rebuild itself, Jason found that he was standing way up high on a motorway bridge.

Ash-grey asphalt stretched on in both directions.

Forests lined the area surrounding.

Cars hummed on their way beneath the bridge.

And then he saw Fiona.

She stood over on the other side of the bridge.

Her back to Jason.

She clung to the rail and stared down at the constantly moving traffic below.

Jason could feel it right down to his bones—call it the Channellers' instinct.

He knew she was going to jump.

Fiona's blond hair flowed back over her shoulders.

Even just observing her in profile, Jason could tell that the brisk wind had brought out a certain redness in her cheeks.

Brought *blood* to the surface of her skin.

Despite the blowing wind, Jason was surprised by the strength of his voice—how he managed to project it above and beyond the elements.

"Isn't this the part where you tell me how I can help you? Who you were on your way to meet?" He swallowed hard. "Who you wanted to say *goodbye* to?"

Fiona didn't turn right away.

Jason was certain, for a span of several seconds, that she would simply ignore him.

That she would simply jump anyway.

But—against Jason's expectations—she did finally turn to face him.

Her eyelids drooped down low.

Her complexion was all at once red raw and deathly pale.

Any humour that'd might've existed in the world was duly snuffed out.

Jason realised now that this was serious.

And that it would be his toughest challenge yet.

Old Mother Time really did know just how to keep Jason on the tips of his toes.

"Do you," Jason said, no smile on his lips any longer, "I mean, you have, uh, *no one?*"

Fiona froze her eyes onto Jason's.

He felt her gaze touch him down at the pit of his stomach.

Fiona looked away from Jason.

She turned her attention—*all* her attention—to the traffic flowing by below.

That gave Jason a fresh tingle in his gut.

Right at that second, Fiona seemed likely to take that pair of fatal steps backward. To throw herself over the edge. Down to her sure-fire doom below.

But then she froze.

She sighed something out.

In a single, gradual, *smooth* motion—one of those which Jason, had he been a little more poetically inclined, might've called a *feminine* motion—Fiona took a pair of steps backward and then she turned right the way around.

Without another word, she crossed the road.

Halted before him.

Close enough to touch if she—or *he*—so wished.

"You don't understand," Fiona said, "to be somewhere else— to be somewhere you don't belong"—here she shook her head —"I do not expect you to understand, on the contrary, I do not believe that you would ever quite understand the extent of the loneliness."

This was the part where Jason simply wanted to scream out at her that he understood perfectly.

But he knew he couldn't reach her.

He had no way with words as she did.

How could he ever express what *he* felt?

"When I first arrived here," Fiona continued, "I wanted new experiences, and that was what I received. But, at times, all of the time, it seemed that there was nobody around who I could relate to—who could relate to *me*."

She paused for a long moment before continuing.

"And then came the news—the *bad* news, the worst news of my life."

Jason was struck by her matter-of-fact tone.

"My parents—they were *killed*."

A pause, then Jason prompted her to continue. "How?" he said.

"A car crash," Fiona replied.

She took a sharp breath.

One of those which indicated she might be on the point of crying.

But she held back the floodgates.

For now.

"When I came to this country," she said, "to this university, I believed that it would be a new kind of stage for me—a chance to see the world differently, do you understand?"

Jason nodded.

"But—coming here, the loneliness, you must understand, it was too much for *me* to bear. It was only on the evening when I received the phone call from my grandfather, that my parents had . . . had been *killed*, that I realised there was no other option." She shook her head. "There was nobody to speak with, not even my neighbours in the university halls."

There was a long, drawn-out silence and then Jason decided he would be the one to break it. "Which block do you . . . *did* you live in?"

She held still.

He could hear her breathing.

And then she told him.

It was Jason's block.

SO CLOSE, SO FAR

At first Jason felt nothing. And then he felt a tingling sensation at the base of his gut.

All of a sudden, it was like his heart and lungs had caught fire.

Before he could think straight at all, he said, "Which floor did you live on?"

Fiona held herself still.

Jason could make out the vaguest of watery films gathering over the surface of her eyeballs. She wasn't far from breaking out into uncontrollable sobs.

Even Jason's computer-sodden brain could see that.

"The second floor," Fiona finally replied.

" 'The second floor'," Jason repeated, and then, because he couldn't stop himself, he said, "I live on the first floor."

"Room 203."

"I live in room 103."

. . . So, there it was, then, Jason had lived in the room right below Fiona's.

And yet he had never—*not even once*—seen her in his life before.

But, then again, Jason hardly set foot outside his room.

Was it any wonder they had never 'bumped' into one another?

Jason was surprised to see that Fiona was smiling when he, again, met her eye. He hadn't expected that. Not with the frost of death lingering in the air—freezing anything and everything that might occupy the space between them.

"Please," Fiona said, "do not worry, not about me, there was nothing at all that you might have done, that you could have said, to change my mind."

Beneath them, the *hum* of car engines continued to flow by.

And it almost felt as if their droning, never-ending drawl, was burrowing its way in through Jason's skull.

Fiona took a couple of steps away from him . . . not toward the railing of the bridge, but along the pavement which edged the side of this motorway overpass.

Jason walked along beside her, attempting to decipher the exact focus of Fiona's gaze.

But, try as he might, he could not see what she saw, and he got an odd feeling that—perhaps—he never would.

They walked off the overpass and up an overgrown, grassy bank, frosted over now.

Fiona led Jason onward at a determined pace, never looking back over her shoulder to check whether or not he was following her.

As Jason stumbled for, like, the millionth time, he pondered just why he did follow. The answer was plain, and it was simple. He had promised Fiona—back in the bus-station waiting room —that he would help her.

And he knew—whatever it might mean to Jason in the Real World—that he could no longer eschew what he had developed to be his *purpose*.

Quite simply, he needed to seek out some sort of peace for Fiona . . . otherwise she would remain lost forever, trapped in this void—for want of a better word—which occupied the space between the Now and the Everafter.

And, as they passed up the grassy bank, emerged on the very edge of what was surely—in the light of day—a stretched-out meadow, but which, now, with snowflakes drifting down and slowly sticking to the already frosted long grasses, seemed almost like another plane altogether.

An *ethereal* plane.

Could this be it?

Could this be the end of life as Jason knew it?

On the horizon, he was sure he could see a low-hanging moon.

Its yellowish, bright glow caused the frosted long grasses to sparkle.

And Fiona was headed for the light.

She had slowed her pace now. It was no longer a challenge for Jason to keep up with her, and as he did, he spoke what words he could. "What is this? What's going to happen next?"

Fiona continued to tread forward into the light and, from somewhere deep within, Jason seemed to finally understand what was happening here.

"You're leaving, aren't you?" Jason said. "I mean, you're moving on, for good."

Fiona replied to him wearing a half smile. She continued her trudge forward entirely unaffected by what Jason had said. The *gravity* of what it was that he had said. "There is nothing for me in the Spiritual Past—nothing at all which might console me."

Her response rendered Jason speechless for several more steps. The light became brighter still. He felt the burn of the white glow on the backs of his eyelids. Suddenly he could smell sulphur, thick on the air, and—at the same time—*honey*.

That last realisation sent Jason bounding down Memory Lane, back when he was in school and had chomped his way, unwittingly, through a honey sandwich his mother had packed in his lunchbox that day.

An innocent mix-up.

What was supposed to be Jason's dad's lunch.

At first, Jason had felt that overwhelmingly hot, sticky sensation in his mouth.

His chest had tightened.

Breathing became impossible.

And the world had gone black.

He had woken up in a hospital bed.

Machines all beeping and grumbling and grinding about him.

Jason could probably pin *that* particular day as the exact moment when he had lost his faith in the world—in the *Real* World.

An allergy which'd jumped up and bit him.

Maybe … maybe … he found himself thinking as the light became far too bright to bear … *this is where I've been heading my entire life …*

maybe my place within this world is to be beyond it—to be one step removed from it. Perhaps I've misled myself my entire life until this point. Maybe this . . . this Everafter is the answer I've searched for my entire life.

Maybe.

The light became so utterly overwhelming and Jason's thoughts scattered so disparately that it was almost a sensation of drowning.

Of coming *close* to drowning.

No way out.

Just, simply, no way out.

Not now.

Within the confines of Jason's own mind—or did she speak right into his ear, her lips brushing against his lobe?—Jason heard Fiona's voice.

One last time.

"Turn back," she said, "it is not too late for you—it is too late for me."

Jason's mind froze.

He could already feel his physical body being torn apart.

His flesh melting freely and easily.

Right off his bones.

But something—*something within him*—just wouldn't allow him to let go. He reached out, clutched tight to Fiona's arm, and whispered to her, in her ear, "Wait, I have an idea."

HOPE IN THE DARK

A *lthough Jason* had never quite allowed the darkness all the way in—*all* the way in—he did so then because he knew it was the only way to escape the blinding white light which might be just as deadly.

Just as willing to pry him from his mortal coil.

He held tight to Fiona's arm. He could feel the calloused tips of his fingers digging into her soft skin. He could feel the two of them being whisked away. Not wanting to sound totally trite, but having no other real frame of reference, he couldn't quite deny that it felt almost—*almost*—as if the two of them were being carried away on the wings of an angel.

Or angels, *plural* . . .

Soon enough, though, Jason felt his and, by extension, Fiona's feet return to reasonably solid ground.

Tarmac.

The snow was gone.

No more of the iciness which'd snagged the air.

A ray of sunlight pierced the brooding clouds above.

It was golden, and it was warm.

Jason couldn't immediately recall having felt so energised. Only now, standing here in the sunshine, did Jason truly realise just how much of a bitch winter was.

The *British* winter . . .

Jason was still gripping tight to Fiona's arm. He turned to her now. Read the twisted look of both surprise and confusion all smeared across her face. Her soft, gentle fingers wrapped themselves about Jason's own, and he released his firm grip from her forearm.

"This is it," Fiona said, her voice almost cracking and her eyes sparkling with unspilled tears. "This is the place."

As Jason looked out over the tree-spotted landscape, to the warm—*summer?*—sunshine which beamed down on the greenery, he realised that, through some sort of intuition, he had managed to drag the two of them back to some place within Fiona's past.

Her home?

Fiona squeezed Jason's hand and then let go. She trotted off along the shingle path before them, the swift movement of her feet kicking up loose pieces of stone and dirt.

As Jason followed her, he noted how a cool breeze kept the bright, sunny day from becoming stifling. He couldn't help but feel a ripple of positivity throb through him.

He followed her through a dilapidated wooden gate and onward into a lush, vibrant field filled with golden corn.

Even Jason's allergies seemed to stand reverent to the moment.

They gave him peace.

As Jason headed further forward, guided by the gentle *patter* and *scuff* of Fiona's feet over the loose ground, he noted a chalk-white cottage sweep into view just ahead. It had a thatched roof and seemed to grow up and out of the land as if it had always been there.

As if it hadn't been built by human hands.

Jason stopped his approach when he observed Fiona arrive at the white-washed picket fence of the cottage. He didn't want to be an invader here. He needed to give Fiona her much needed space. So she might reunite with her parents without a Channeller breathing down the back of her neck.

And so Jason watched Fiona all the way along the slate slabs which formed the garden path to the bright, navy-blue—*freshly painted?*—front door. He watched as she turned the hefty brass doorknob and eased her way inside without so much as a glance back at him.

Neither did she bother to shut the door behind her.

Jason found himself a comfortable place on a nearby grassy bank. He sat. He absorbed the gleaming blue—*blue*; not grey—sky which spun out above.

He lost all sense of passing time.

As far as he was concerned, he might've sat there on the grassy bank for as short of a time as ten minutes, or for as long as an hour.

In fact, Jason was somewhat surprised when he caught sight of Fiona slipping back out of the front door. He supposed that he had grown so accustomed to his quiet, natural surroundings that he had been able to forget all about the humanity which plagued the surface of the Earth.

Fiona was smiling—*grinning*, really—from ear to ear.

When she walked, her gait seemed to have a certain lightness to it. All at the same time, her steps were heavily placed, and yet, without effort. Her skin shone rosy-red in the bright, summer sunlight.

And she was approaching him.

Jason remained where he was, slumped up on the bank, plucking at the brilliant yellow petals of a dandelion.

Fiona hovered and then she dropped herself down on the bank beside him.

For several moments—*minutes?*—they sat where they were.

In silence.

Finally, Fiona said, "Thank you for bringing me here—I shall never forget this."

Jason met her eye briefly.

He plucked off the final petal of the dandelion and then cast it off into the breeze.

He threw the stem into the long grasses which lay about him.

" 'Never forget', huh?" Jason said. "You'll never have to leave, if you don't want to—this is your Spiritual Past, you know."

Fiona glanced back at Jason. Her eyes seemed to sparkle in the sunlight, and Jason saw Fiona was a different person entirely in the summer.

The winter truly did have a way of knocking the colour out of everything and everyone.

"I won't stay here," Fiona replied.

Jason felt his chest tighten. His heart fluttered up to his throat. "But, I thought this was where you would be happiest. Now you no longer need to suffer the loss of your parents—never need go through the loneliness . . ."

"But it is not real."

Jason couldn't think of an answer to that one right away, so he allowed himself to consider it properly before replying, "But, the alternative?" His voice was fraught with tension now. "We both saw it—that shining, unconscionable light. Who knows where it leads? It might be the gateway to a whole world of pain." He paused for a fraction of a second and then added, "Of loneliness."

Jason couldn't quite tell *when* it had exactly happened, but all he knew was that Fiona was not smiling any longer.

She stared out over the golden fields of corn, to the azure horizon, apparently in contemplation. Finally, she said, "I will not live a lie—I am not capable."

Jason was about to pick holes with her usage of the term 'live', but he had no chance because—right then, without warning or reason—Fiona leaned into him and kissed him full and softly on the mouth.

It felt like Jason's whole body would melt as Fiona pulled back. His mind was so filled with sensation—*longing*—that he nearly lost the word which Fiona spoke.

"Goodbye."

And the whole world just seemed to drift apart.

ANOTHER TIME, ANOTHER LIFE

*J*ason could feel himself floating.

He flurried his legs, looking for any sort of purchase whatsoever.

There was none to find.

He felt varying hot-and-cold sensations.

He seemed to boil from within.

And then *freeze.*

Jason swiped at the air.

Clutching.

Craving.

Grasping nothing.

When he opened his eyes this time, there was not even anything as solid as darkness to be had.

There was simply nothing at all.

Jason wasn't even floating.

Not in the *true* sense of the word.

What this void—or whatever it was—afforded Jason was time to think.

To think about what'd just happened.

How Fiona had kissed him.

Then said goodbye.

Was that it?

Was it all over now?

Would he *ever* manage to find his way home?

Where even *was* his home now?

. . . And he put that question to himself—not in any sort of intangible, navel-gazing way, but in a very real, very geographically sound sense.

As Jason waded out into the nothingness, he began to believe that he saw shapes.

Or maybe it was only symptomatic of a disoccupied mind.

Perhaps, since his mind could not cling to the blank space which surrounded it, it was simply creating its own little fantasy.

Something—*anything*—to cling onto.

Voices ebbed in and out of his mind.

Jason found himself visited by a series of visions—of *memories* —and he lost himself within them all.

He saw Dougleglass.

In his lederhosen.

And Lady Gweniveere.

In her fur coat.

Patrick dressed—*eternally*—in his chicken suit.

As their faces grew within Jason's mind, as remembrance took hold, other shapes formed about them.

First with Dougleglass . . . his long-betrothed appearing beside him.

Both aiming smiles at Jason.

Jason smiled back.

Found himself smiling back.

Unable to help himself.

Lady Gweniveere . . . her lover appearing out of the ethereal veil. The two of them smiled too.

And then—finally—Patrick, with his fiancé.

The two of them, and their glittering eyes, firing their glances right back at Jason.

As Jason felt the tug of his smile begin to cause the sides of his mouth to ache, he couldn't help but wonder—wonder if this, if what he was seeing right now, might be some sort of consolation prize.

Old Mother Time's way of telling him that to have helped *three* at the expense of *one* was no little thing.

But, as Jason felt the smile slipping off his lips, he couldn't help but think—but *know*—that he hadn't done enough.

That he might've done better.

And, as he felt all those faces of the Unquiet he had set free, into their own personal Spiritual Pasts, Jason knew that Fiona— the one who had got away—would haunt him forever more.

There was, quite simply, nothing that could be done about that.

A CHRISTMAS GIFT

I *t all returned* to Jason somewhat suddenly.

The low drawl of music seeping from the busted, metallic-sounding speakers of the bus-station waiting room. The worming throb which now emanated from the—*apparently fixed*—radiators.

That stink of disinfectant.

That dry, *nothing* taste at the back of Jason's throat.

When Jason glanced about the waiting room, he saw that he was alone.

The only one here now.

The only one who still needed to get home.

Only when Jason glanced at the aged screen showing the imminent departures did he realise that it was working again. And that the bus to Staplesham was leaving in barely two minutes' time.

Moving quickly, Jason bent down, snatched up the rucksack

which contained his travelling computer and assorted, randomly selected clothes to get him through the Christmas period, and he swept on out of the waiting room.

Not even stopping for one final look at the place.

At this place which had—somehow—changed his life.

When Jason had first left his room in his university halls that night, it hadn't been on much more than a whim. This vague, gut feeling that, really, he didn't want to spend Christmas in his room.

Alone.

It had been impossible for him to really put his finger on the exact reason why he had felt that way. He had just upped sticks and left.

That simple.

As Jason sat on the deserted bus, a good three quarters back from the driver, he peered on out through the chilly window-pane and wondered what had happened only hours before.

How Fiona had taken that fatal leap off the motorway bridge.

Put an end to her suffering.

Jason wondered—*already*—about the drama which might accompany his return to university after the Christmas break.

There would be a formal letter.

'Support' meetings.

A whole *buzz* of scandal about the whole of Jason's block for maybe a week.

Perhaps two.

And then everybody would forget.

Forget about Fiona.

That was the thing about loneliness, about being unable to count on so much as a single person in the world.

When you were gone—finally gone—there would be nobody to mourn you.

Would there be anybody to mourn Jason if he was to, say, suffer a crash in this bus right now?

His parents, of course.

They would, at least for a while.

But then who?

His course mates?

. . . Not likely, 'mates' was something of a convenient term but it also was a misnomer.

There was nothing 'matey' surrounding Jason's relationship with his course mates . . .

As the bus swept along the backstreets of Staplesham, Jason could make out a few snowflakes floating down on the icy breeze outside. He could make out a choice few settling down onto the frosted pavements, layering the iced-over puddles. He looked over the closed-up shop fronts, to the garish, multi-coloured Christmas lights which hung suspended from high wires, over the street. Flashing away with their golds and greens and silvers and reds.

All festive.

Warming.

. . . So, why did Jason feel so chilled inside?

When the bus pulled up to a halt at the tiny, flimsy wooden structure which passed for Jason's local bus stop, Jason couldn't help wondering just how his bus stop had managed to squeeze through all these years—from when it had served Jason back in secondary school, to now when it served as an off-the-wall home-coming.

Jason thanked the driver and wished him a Merry Christmas, for which Jason received a—rather muted—Merry Christmas right back.

He stepped down onto the unsalted pavement and promptly almost broke his bloody neck.

Thankfully, though, Jason's travelling computer, still nestled within his rucksack, acted as a kind of ballast, keeping him upright.

With a cloud of acrid exhaust, the bus pulled out of the stop and—with surely far more brisk acceleration than it would've put to use if there had still been passengers on board—it vanished around the corner.

In less than ten seconds, even the *rumble* of its engine was a distant memory.

Jason paced along the pavement, both taking care not to slip a second time and catching glances in at the Christmas Eve scenes taking place in the houses which'd not yet drawn their curtains:

Christmas trees.

Twinkling lights.

TV light splashing its glow over gormless families—several of whom clutched glasses of wine, or pints of beer, or flutes of champagne.

Jason had never really got TV.

Everything he could ever need—*entertainment-wise*—he could find on his computer.

Internet included, of course.

It was as Jason approached his own home that he realised,

padding his pockets and then rifling quickly through his bag, that he'd left his keys behind—in his university room.

Trust him . . . trust *him* to do that . . .

Luckily, though, it was Christmas Eve, and his parents would be in.

They always were.

At least for as long as Jason could recall.

When Jason reached the sturdy, wooden fencepost which marked the beginning of his parents' front drive, he paused.

He caught that—somehow familiar—prickling sensation at the back of his neck.

And then it moved downward.

To his shoulders.

Worked its way down his spine.

On instinct, Jason spun around.

He thought it was a mirage.

If mirages were even *possible* on a snowy night.

Were they?

But there she stood.

Across the street.

As real as Jason himself.

As real as Jason was going to *get*.

Fiona.

She was smiling vaguely at him and she carried her own ruck-sack dangling over her shoulder.

Jason doubted her rucksack's prime purpose would be to house a travelling computer like his was.

Fiona glanced to her left.

Then her right.

She crossed the street.

Before Jason could quite comprehend what was happening, she stood beside him.

He could feel her body warmth emanate through the air.

It breathed life into his iced-over skin—skin which, until now, until this very moment, he had considered to be normal.

But when Fiona was near, he felt a tingling sensation pass across the surface of his skin.

His heart pounded just a little harder.

She was here.

Questions bounced about Jason's mind so quickly that he had little-to-no hope of stopping them—or even making sense of them.

But maybe sense was overrated.

Perhaps he should just speak with his heart.

. . .Not to get too bogged down with clichés.

"Are you," Jason began. "Are you . . . *real?*"

Fiona reached out for his hand.

Her flesh was bright pink from the cold and, when she answered him, breath poured out through her lips as steam. "Yes," she said, "I am real."

"But," Jason replied, "I don't get it at all. I thought that you, that it was . . ."

Fiona's smile and the touch of her soft skin against Jason's cheek was enough to shut him up so that she could explain.

"Old Mother Time said that diligent Channellers, such as yourself, can benefit at this time of year, if they are only willing to help others."

"I . . . I . . ."

"Shh," Fiona replied, now holding her index finger to Jason's lips, "she thought that I—that *we*—deserved another chance, one more opportunity for us both to be happy. For us to see off our loneliness."

And here Fiona leaned forward and kissed Jason hard on the mouth.

This kiss was totally different from the one with which she had wished Jason goodbye.

Whereas before, Jason could feel her retreating from him —*lost forever*—even as their lips had first touched; this time Fiona only pushed harder into him, urging him to embrace her.

And Jason did.

He held her there in his arms until the two of them shivered from the cold.

Suddenly self-conscious, Jason glanced up and then down the street.

And he saw her.

Duffel coat.

Face steeped in shadow.

Hands stuffed in pockets.

But—*unmistakeably*—her.

Old Mother Time.

As if she had only put in an appearance so that Jason might see her standing there, at the end of the street, she turned her back on Fiona and Jason both, and then disappeared around the corner.

Lost beneath the heavy snowfall.

The snow which fell even harder than before.

Jason turned his attention back to Fiona—now shaking even harder in his arms, then he said, "I guess you've got nowhere to be for Christmas, then?"

Even as Jason uttered that not-even-a-joke, he regretted having said it.

He was supposed to be *sensitive* to others' thoughts and feelings.

But—*thankfully*—Fiona only smiled back at him.

Jason supposed that he could pick up all the subtleties of Polite Society as he went along.

In this relationship.

"No," Fiona replied, "nowhere to go."

Jason glanced back to the front door of his parents' home and he felt another tingle pass through him. "I have to warn you," he said, "my parents aren't expecting me, let alone *company*."

"It is okay," Fiona said, "I assure you that I can be quite charming."

And, with only another second's hesitation—to check for any further sign of Old Mother Time over his shoulder; there wasn't —Jason led Fiona by the hand up the garden path to his parents' front door.

As Jason stood there, on the doorstep, he speculated that he had never before been this happy in his life. This was it. This was living.

No more loneliness.

And so he walked through the door.

They *both* walked through the door.

THE END

AUTHOR'S NOTE

Thank you for taking the time to read one of my books. If you would like to hear about my latest releases you can sign up for my newsletter here: www.raymondsflex.com

Thanks for reading!

Raymond S Flex

A Candle, A Kiss, A Christmas Gift
A Novel

Copyright © Raymond S Flex, 2015.
Published by DIB Books
All rights reserved.

Cover design and layout copyright © DIB Books, 2015.
Cover art copyright © Krivosheev Vitaly / Shutterstock, 2015.

www.ingramcontent.com/pod-product-compliance
Lightning Source LLC
Chambersburg PA
CBHW031229260626
47169CB00007B/2212